The Panic Button

Beer at the movies!

Thanx so much for everything!

—Koom

The Panic Button

Koom Kankesan

QUATTRO BOOKS

The publication of *The Panic Button* has been generously supported by the Canada Council for the Arts and the Ontario Arts Council.

Cover design: Diane Mascherin
Author's photo: Shira Palansky
Typography: Grey Wolf Typography
Editor: Luciano Iacobelli

Library and Archives Canada Cataloguing in Publication

Kankesan, Koom
    The panic button / Koom Kankesan.

ISBN 978-1-926802-30-5

    I. Title.

PS8621.A55P36 2011   C813'.6   C2010-907659-1

Novella Series #16
Published by Quattro Books Inc.
89 Pinewood Avenue
Toronto, Ontario, M6C 2V2
www.quattrobooks.ca

Printed in Canada

To Holly McCuaig

1

Who the fuck would want to marry me? That's the first thing that crosses my mind when my mother mentions marriage. She brings it up at least once a day; it's the water torture method of persuasion. *Marriage!... Marriage!... Marriage!...* As you can see, due to the cast on my leg, I can't get very far from the drops.

One of these days, that final drop of water is going to split my head right open, cleave my brain in two. Then, I, like all the other sad Tamil losers, will shuffle forward and wait to be matched with our counterparts, and we'll all have a big wedding. Won't it be grand? Our brains will be cut apart with our parents' scalpels, then fused together with our mates'. We'll all have four hemispheres, two cortexes, and one mind. Arranged marriages are the panic button of Hindu romance. How long can I hold out? In a few months, I'll hit thirty and my hand will waver over the button, just like everybody else. My parents, especially my mother, assure me that this will be the case. But I'm still young, doctor. There's hope for me, right? Tell me it's not too late to meet someone and catch up. Tell me that there are others like me out there. But like I say – who the fuck would want to marry me?

I know that you have to write a report. I know that your technique involves listening. Like a white lab coat, like a blank wall, you listen and don't say anything. I know you won't tell me what you think. But I'm supposed to convince you I'm okay, fit to flow back to the real world, present a version that'll make it easy to sign off your form. Put your pen down for a second; listen to my story and tell me what I should do. Because it doesn't ultimately matter what your report says if I'm irreparably cracked...if the bone around the hole in my ankle grows back and the fracture lines recede, what does that matter if the ragged hole in my heart, hidden, remains?

My story goes back to my parents. They were married in the traditional way, not knowing each other. Eight years apart in age. It's a wonder that they were able to get along. That they touched each other or made love. That they were able to figure things out in that repressed, depersonalized age so long ago. And to have two kids. My parents' generation was oppressed by arranged marriages. No individuality, no choice. My own generation is oppressed by the dating game. How to speak to each other, how to act?

Who is there to teach us these things? The white people had it in their blood. It seeped in over generations. Even if their parents didn't teach them how to make love, they picked it up from the TV, the magazines, the schoolyard, the very air. Our parents turned off the TV or changed the channel whenever characters began to kiss. To shame us. To embarrass us for life – and it has worked.

My mother walks around saying, "If you can't find someone, I'll find someone for you." Thanks, mom. Don't get me wrong – I love you, mother. But did you give me a head start or any advice in this terrible game? Since puberty, it's been hell to figure out women and what to do with them, and I could use a little understanding. You married someone you hardly knew because your family urged you to, popped out a couple of kids, and then never saw him again for years. What could you possibly know about marriage?

I should tell you now that they're not divorced. Far from it. After all, we're Tamils – that would *never* be an option. A year after the war broke out in Sri Lanka, after my grandparents' farm was burned down and their house vandalized, my parents made the decision to leave everything and run. If they went through the immigration and naturalization process, it would have taken years, it would never have happened. Their solution, like that of many others, was to have themselves smuggled into another country and apply their claims as refugees. My mother left with Roshan and myself when I was three and he was seven. We ended up in Scarborough. My father was supposed to follow but the agency (they always call them 'agencies' and not 'human smugglers') screwed him over. He got dropped off in Nigeria, then Germany, and finally, failingly, ended up back home. We, on the other hand, stayed with relatives in a cramped apartment and then got a cramped apartment of our own. I had a small bed in my mother's room beside hers while Roshan slept on a fold-out couch. It would be years before we could afford a two bedroom apartment. My mother worked and raised us, cleaning office suites overnight and various other things that don't involve much English. I almost cry when I think of the things she did. I know that if I were put in the same position, I'd break. But when she and my dad talk about marriage, personal things they know nothing about, it makes me angry. She talks brazenly to friends and other fools as if she has the right – as if the reason I'm single is not in large part due to them.

Listen, there was a time in high school, grade ten, there was this girl that I liked. What was her name? It doesn't matter. I liked her so much I pushed through my shyness in class and talked to her. She even liked me a little bit, I think. We began working together on school projects and such. There was a presentation in Latin class that we had to rehearse and she wanted me to come over to her house. I said I would but I felt uneasy – I didn't know what my mother would say and I kept on delaying asking for permission until I finally reasoned that I'd better go and either not tell Amma or just tell her afterwards. It's easier to ask for forgiveness than permission, right? Anyway, everything was set up and then the girl called our apartment, assuming my mother knew. Amma answered and when she realized what was going on, went through the roof. I mean, she literally started screaming and banging the receiver against the wall. That was it as far as that girl went.

At Christmas, I bought the girl a Christmas card as a way of apology. I wrote a message telling her what a great person she was but when I got to the bottom, I didn't know how to sign it. I wanted to sign it 'xoxoxo' (hugs and kisses) because I still liked her a little bit but then I thought that might make her uncomfortable. I thought of taking the kisses out so I was just sending her the hugs but I couldn't figure out which were the hugs and which were the kisses. Since xo's are hugs and kisses, it would make sense for the x's to be hugs and the o's to be kisses. But if you send someone a note and just sign it 'xxx', it suggests something explicit. 'ooo' doesn't seem right either. In the end, I just threw out the card.

See, this is what having a Tamil mom will do for you.

2

I can barely remember that first plane ride. The massive jump across the Atlantic from London to Pearson Terminal Three. It's quite the experience, quite the jolt. Coming through those gates with forged passports and little else except the clothes on your back. All the immigrants waiting to meet their relatives, newer immigrants. The size of the terminal arches, smell of sweat and stale breath beside the luggage conveyors, all the people and the lines. In 1983, it was possible to squeak through with false papers and shifty-eyed determination. It was possible to fall upon the kindness of sympathetic customs guards. They understood our persistence and desperation, despite our lack of English; we were from another country that did not have their comforts and protections. How times have changed!

Roshan remembers it a lot better than I do. We stayed with relatives of relatives for two years, hoping and expecting our father to arrive any day. We looked forward to his arrival as if, with it, our fortunes would turn around. My earliest memories are of that too-cramped apartment, my mother and I in one room and the other family with their baby forced to cram themselves into another. The cockroaches in the apartment would find their way into the fridge. We lined up in turns to use the bathroom. If the landlord dropped by, we pretended not to be home. But I also remember eating food together around the table and watching our first Western TV shows – *Wheel of Fortune* and *Knight Rider*. Seeing snow fall and stay on the ground for the first time. My first memories are from this time and I can't say that they're all bad. In the few photos we have from then, I'm smiling. Roshan has suddenly become the reluctant man of our little family. At the tender age of seven, he is sleeping on a fold-out bed.

After the first year, when the agency had shipped our father back to Sri Lanka instead of bringing him here, my mother decided that she'd better take matters into her own hands. She worked in a calendar factory during the day and cleaned offices at night. What a way to live! She hardened her heart, pursed her lips, and went to work. I remember her absences, her coming home late at night, long after I was supposed to be asleep, the tired shuffle of her cracked soles, and her sighs. The strange thing is that I don't remember anything of my father or my time in Sri Lanka before the flight. My earliest memories of my father are a disembodied voice on the phone, a scratchy, weak connection, the hot hum and buzz of the Sri Lankan air behind him.

Imagine what it was like for Roshan. It was okay for me because I grew up here. Roshan came here with very little English. I adapted quickly but the homesickness and the awkward unfamiliarity must have stayed with him a long time. Imagine turning eight in somebody else's apartment and instead of a Transformers lunchbox or whatever, receiving a plaid shirt because that's all our mother could afford – bare essentials. Imagine being nine and not having any friends at school because most of the kids are white and play hockey or go ice skating. Imagine being in high school and not owning a single Vuarnet or Beaver Canoe sweatshirt to show off at school, just the same old plaid shirts and grey sweaters. No idea how to make friends or what to say. Roshan would not meet or make any friends like himself until he went to university.

He was serious and studious – he had done well at school and that was his claim to an identity back home. The aunts and uncles, and even the kids, had cooed over him – he was known as a smart boy, organized, and on top of his schoolwork. That'll get you nothing over here. His confidence slipped and faltered, and if you ask me, never quite recovered. He hardly comes to visit my mother anymore. Gone are the days when he used to dutifully massage my mother's feet. I've never been able to do that myself, to kowtow so completely. Despite our differences, my mother respects me more so for this. It's not fair. As men, we're encouraged to not show any weaknesses, except to devote ourselves to our parents. But perhaps this is the ultimate test? How are we to pass, to earn their approval and their respect all in one go?

In our culture, men are men and sometimes, women are also men. Our mother became tough, transformed herself from the beleaguered woman who had crossed with us, to a leathery wizened wizard. We moved into our own apartment and it was her doing. We listened to her on the phone with our Appa, her voice and stature grown in size, and it was not her. She spoke to him frankly, perhaps in a way that he had never been spoken to before. Afterwards, the new apartment would feel overheated and baked with tension, a kiln that had not been aired. I remember her shaking her head once after such a phone call and muttering, "What does he think we're doing here? Living like kings and queens?" Roshan and I did not say anything. Our father tried to come over once more, through the agency, but things went wrong. Years later, my mother tried to bring him over legally but he screwed up the interview. At least that's what she said.

Roshan went to university and became an accountant. I followed, and somehow, ambiguously, passed through a business program with a sprinkling of humanities. If you ask me why I did that, I wouldn't be able to tell you now. Neither of us left home. To leave was a desire that built up in Roshan and only found its vent years later. I thought of it myself but couldn't bear to leave my mother, all alone, to smother in that apartment, abandoned and forsaken. Settled in a sedate job at a minor corporation, Roshan made his move. He was in his mid thirties and Amma had been bothering him about marriage. Proposals and inquiries came in from places as distant as the Southern States and Australia.

Since I've mentioned it before, you're maybe wondering 'who the fuck would want to marry Roshan?' Well, he's an accountant, very staid, very predictable. He respects both his mother and father, acts like a proper Tamil. He may not be diamonds but he's at least cubic zirconia. You've got to remember – as a young child, he excelled in school. Somehow, the same set of smarts didn't transfer to Canada. His grades were good, if not great, but something was missing. As if, perpetually, he was never quite sure where he was; instead of developing new social skills, he crawled into a shell looking for others' approval. Our mother, in the process of finding a new, hardier, more resourceful version of herself, was not the person to give him that approval. He floated along like an unshaped piece of wood until he finished school and settled into his modest career. He suddenly found himself in official adulthood. Inquiries about marriage started trickling in. My mother even met with a couple of go-betweens before Roshan knew about them. This was one of the most important things she would ever do for her son and she had very high expectations with regards to dowry and the terms and conditions of matrimony.

Lakshmi was a girl who worked in the office of a friend of Roshan's. An employee of one of his engineer or doctor friends. She had finished a degree in sociology. Lakshmi was introduced formally to Roshan but he didn't say anything to Amma for a long time. He took Lakshmi out, met her parents, and got to know her discreetly, which is a feat in our household. When he finally announced her existence and their engagement a year ago, Amma went through the roof. How could a son of hers go behind her back like this when she had worked so hard for that very son? Roshan had done the unthinkable – he had sided with the girl's family and prepped them for our mother's reaction. He had foregone the dowry. Gone was the pleasure of the viewing where my mother and her friends would go inspect the girl. Lakshmi has never formally served tea to our mother. Amma was furious. But Roshan had pulled the ultimate coup. He had phoned our father independently, appraised him of the situation, and flattered him by allowing Appa to make the final decision. Pleased at having some say over anything, especially something so important, from his current place of impotence, our father approved. He approved without having spoken to the girl or her family, and without even having seen a photo.

Lakshmi is flighty and bubbly; she is breezy yet fearsome. Though Tamil like us, she has no problem asserting herself and her wants directly. An only child, her parents have pampered her. They are well-to-do and she has not been in want of anything. Why did Roshan do it? Was it the panic button? It gets to all of us. Did he wake up in the middle of the night in shivers and a cold sweat? Did he slam the button down, welding his palm to the console, afraid to let up even after the siren started shrieking?

3

You want to know how the whole mess began? It was Amma's fifty-fourth birthday and Roshan and Lakshmi decided to take her to a South Asian restaurant on the Saturday instead of the day itself. I was supposed to go on a coffee date with a woman I'd met on the internet. This was the first time I'd meet this woman in the flesh. With two days notice, Roshan and Lakshmi announced that they were going to take my mother out to dinner in Richmond Hill, where Lakshmi lived. I politely asked if they could reschedule. Like the heartless bastards they were, they said, "Why? What's so important that you can't make Amma's birthday?" I couldn't very well tell them that I had a date, so I unhappily agreed to go and then left a message for the woman asking if *we* could reschedule. She replied with a text on the Saturday, quite curt, asking me "why bother?" I swear, I hate communicating through computers even though my job involves being glued to one. Why do I even bother with internet dating? Fraught with indignity and humiliation, there must be better ways for a person to be let down.

So there I was, unhappy, sitting beside my mother in the back seat, on the way to the restaurant, while Roshan drove and his fiancée navigated from shotgun. Amma wasn't too pleased either. She wrapped her duffel coat around herself tightly and dug back into the seat as the highway flashed past us. "Her name means fortune but she's brought us anything but," muttered my mother, so softly that only I could hear, and pointing her chin at Lakshmi. It seemed as if there was a fifth ghostly presence in the car with us, sitting between Amma and myself: Appa, her husband. Who knew where he was right now? What he was doing?

Tamil customers were scattered here and there in the restaurant, but it was not busy. This place was owned, run, and frequented by first-generation immigrants. There wasn't much in the way of table service. All the usual South Asian curries and staples were laid out at the buffet and we were expected to serve ourselves.

Lakshmi, unnecessarily, served us all.

"You shouldn't have done that, Lakshmi," said my mother, frowning and pulling her coat tightly around herself, "I prefer to serve myself." She beckoned to the sole waiter and cashier to bring her a tea.

"Are you cold, Amma?" asked Roshan, pulling at the shirt sleeves under his diamond patterned sweater. He could tell that Lakshmi was upset at Amma's attitude towards her. Since Roshan never stands up for her to Amma, this made things worse. In fact, insisting on marrying Lakshmi was the first big thing that I can remember him taking a stand on. Taking a firm stand on this battle seemed to exhaust him for all the small, petty fights that followed. But he never sides against Lakshmi either; she has him wrapped around her finger. He sweats like a teabag when he's between her and Amma. Out of the frying pan and into the fire. Out of the kettle and into the teacup. It's not his fault. Amma coddled Roshan when it came to making the big decisions about his life. If he's weak and stuffy in situations that require teeth, it's her fault. And then she criticizes him no end as an adult. Amma just tugged on the collars of her coat and stirred the frothy tea that the waiter brought for her.

"Let's give her the present," said Lakshmi.

They pulled out a gift bag with a large card in the shape of a star taped to the front of it. 'Happy Birthday' yelled the card, 'You're Only as Young as You Feel!' Shouldn't it have read 'You're Only as Old as You Feel'? Which one sounds less depressing? They handed it over to my mother, now fifty-four years old/young. She had Roshan when she was twenty years old, fourteen years younger than Roshan was then. Can you believe it? She would have married when she was nineteen.

How old was our father? Twenty-seven. I was born four long years after Roshan. What happened during those intervening years? Another three years later, we were smuggled out of the country and shipped in a smelly freighter's hold with my mother and brother to East Africa and then to London, before flying here. There was no more coddling after that. Roshan says that he can remember a few things from that time. The darkness, dampness, cramp, and fear in the hold. Me crying. Waiting for hours in people's back yards. The feel and colour of orange tic tacs that some stranger gave us. Watching an old Biblical movie on a black and white TV. I don't remember too much. My earliest memories are Canadian. I couldn't tell you what our father smelled like or felt like. Or even looked like. Sometimes I think I remember the shape of him, as through the haze of a dream upon waking. Not really though. I feel as if I remember him going out to work early and returning late in the day, over the government roads, rough and pebbly with tar, on his bicycle. The slow way he would remove his belt and the wild hair, full of sand and sweat, upon the beaches of Colombo. Over the years, on the phone, he's been loud and distant at the same time, wiry and irate. At what point did my mother lose her youth and lightheartedness to take on these characteristics herself? I watched her then, stirring her tea in the restaurant.

Inside Roshan and Lakshmi's bag, with a big blue bow on it, was a blender. My mother picked it out and threw away the bow. "What am I supposed to do with this?" she asked.

"Amma, you can make smoothies with it!" cried Lakshmi, perhaps too overenthusiastically. Can you picture Roshan's fiancée? She's chubby like him, has a piping voice that some find sweet, others find whiny and overcompensating, long black hair; in other words the kind of girl who is the opposite of Roshan and the same thing as him at the same time. He in his diamond patterned sweaters, robust belly, and thick spectacles. My mother's disapproval continuously making him anxious.

Anyway, Lakshmi was expounding the virtues of blending: "...you can crush ice cubes in it and blend fruits and vegetables. You can juice, you can make purees."

"What did you get me, Thambi?" Amma asked me. Thambi's not my name. It's Tamil for 'little brother'. Roshan started calling me that when we were very little and it's stuck – nobody uses my real name anymore. Everybody calls me Thambi, even the people I work with.

I pulled out an envelope with some cash in it. I won't tell how much; I think that's distasteful. Anyway, I learned a long time ago that money is the most practical, versatile gift for all occasions where my mother is concerned. What can you get that lady? Anything you get is bound to be met with incredulity or disappointment, if not both. I handed over the envelope which had 'Happy Birthday, Amma' printed on it in magic marker. My mother tore it open, carefully counted the notes, and pocketed them.

"Lakshmi and I have another present for you," said Roshan. He pulled out an envelope with a piece of paper in it. My mother took it from him and she had to fumble with her spectacles for a moment. Pursed lips moved slightly as she scanned the paper.

"What is this?" she asked.

"Can't you guess?" asked Lakshmi, a gleam in her eyes, the look of a predator when it knows it has finally, exasperatingly, won its prey.

"Lakshmi's parents and I have been putting away money," said Roshan. "We've been in contact with Appa and an agency. We're going to do it right this time. We're finally going to bring him over!"

Lakshmi put an arm around Roshan. A finger of hers brushed against his lips and he almost sucked on it with excitement. I don't mean that to sound too sexual. The thought of the two of them going at it, him like a beached whale and her like some scuba diver who's accidentally speared him, is not something I think about. But I can tell you this – they had performed a coup. They had finally won. The struggle to beat down the last of my mother's resistance was over, and they knew it.

Amma was shocked. She tore her glasses off her face, then clapped her thin wavering hands together and screamed. So I guess it was a good thing. She reached out of her coat and clasped Lakshmi by the girl's face. They stood up, Lakshmi's face radiant, my mother shaking. People at other tables stared at us briefly. They could guess what was going on. Mother and future daughter-in-law gasped as if with one breath. Roshan pushed his glasses above the bridge of his nose and resumed eating.

"I have to talk to your father about this – it's so soon," said Amma.

"I hope Appa will be happy!" gasped Lakshmi.

If I knew Lakshmi, she was making it seem like a done deal when it wasn't, using it to leverage my mother's happiness. A chain of desired events would follow. Mortgage first. Matching sofas and bedsheets second. "Well, I would have liked it if you had talked to me about it first...anyway, good news is good news...now I only have one wish left," said my mother, putting her hand to her heart.

"Here we go," I muttered.

"And that's to see my second son settled with somebody. Thambi, why can't you be like Roshan? He has a nice job, a nice fiancée!"

"I'm fine with my job, ma, everything's fine. Leave me alone."

She pinched my cheek, knowing full well how I hate it. "How can I help it if I worry about my youngest the most?"

"We're right here, Amma, we can hear you," said Roshan.

Later in the car, the women: fed, plump, and happy in the backseat, arms around each other. My mother giving Lakshmi advice on rearing children: "It's best to discipline them with a firm hand – set the rules early if you want to keep trouble away. Don't make the same mistake I made with these two."

Mind you, I'm in the front with Roshan, listening to this. "Oh, Amma, you always pretend to be tougher than you are – we all know it," I say.

"Well, it's worked, hasn't it?"

Roshan is quiet. He doesn't say anything and I wonder what he's thinking. All the years and distance between us and here we are sitting side by side in the car before his marriage, and there's nothing to say. Him with all his pent-up frustration and dutiful rage, beating me up when we were little kids to take it out. Until I am five and kick him and hit him back, and I learn that I can do this. He cowered and left me alone after that, developed his permanent stoop. Roshan's older than I am but I haven't thought of him as my older brother for a long time. I don't respect him or his choices; part of me is secretly glad that he has chosen to get married because it deflects the pressure away from me. It also paradoxically draws more attention to me and my wayward status. In the car, I have a sick feeling in my stomach because, before the wedding is over, I will have to give him something of myself that I do not want to give; I will have to pretend to be something I am not. It's amazing what little bits and pieces I remember, as if they're happening right now, like fragments of glass and bone being whisked away by the wind, in the wake of the car on the highway.

"Since Appa's not here yet, you'll have to help me set up everything and invite everybody," said my mother dreamily, looking at the back of my neck.

"Any chance that we can make a push, try to get him here before the wedding?" asked Lakshmi, in her newfound seat of power in our family.

"That man? With his luck? Not a chance," snorted my mother, a little bit more harshly than was called for.

After that, silence reigned while Roshan drove.

Roshan turned to me. "Although we'll be having a Hindu wedding and all," he began.

"And we'll invite everybody! They'd better come!" emphasized my mother.

"Though we'll be having a Hindu wedding," said Roshan, "I want you to be like my best man. I want to have a bachelor night, respectable of course. I want you to plan it."

"Bachelor event," corrected Lakshmi, "you're not staying out all night. And I can help you with the planning, Thambi."

Great. I've never been close to Roshan, so why me? That's just what I needed, on top of everything. Him expecting the impossible and her riding my shoulders like the old man in that Sinbad story. Hearts as big as subway tokens, those two.

When we got home, after dropping Lakshmi off and an operatic and touching farewell between her and Roshan, the red eye of the answering machine blinked furiously. Our father had left not one but two messages. My mother listened to them without taking her coat off and then picked up the phone, pulled her calling card out, and dialed the numbers. All of the excitement of the last two hours flooded out of her, through her sensible shoes into the ground, and she seemed suddenly tired. Roshan went to sleep in our room but I waited up with the lights out until she finished her conversation. She finally came into the kitchen a few minutes later.

"Your father's going to be here for the wedding," she said. Her voice was strained and ambiguous. In the dark, I could not tell what passed over her face.

4

Work used to be an escape from the pressures at home. Not lately. Our company is a small marketing firm in the entertainment district. I didn't know it at the time I interviewed, but everyone else who works there, besides Gerry, our manager, is a woman. Gerry's never out of his office, down among the troops, so I'm surrounded by a sea of estrogen. Estrogen that takes itself much too seriously. I was hired as the 'IT' guy because of my business degree. That makes a lot of sense, right? Next to these women, who don't know how to do anything except turn their computers on and check Facebook, I'm a whiz. I can format a hard drive, manage a local network, and install programs. Apparently that's all it takes to keep a contract around here. To round me out, they've got me answering webmail.

The space, a warehouse loft with white walls and grey cubicles, is slowly being outfitted with Macs. This will make me doubly redundant. Gerry stands in his glass box office above us and watches. Do I stand out amongst all the women to him, or disappear as one of little interest? How long before he realizes I am unnecessary? I have to attend our product launches and make sure the projectors and whatever fancy gimmicky ideas they set up don't break down. This was the case with the new product we were launching at the time: the Nipple. If you don't remember it, and why would you?, the Nipple was a gimmicky PDA (phone/planner/internet console) developed by a Montreal firm trying to cash in on the social networking craze. It took its audacious name from the way it was meant to look like a stylized breast. It actually celebrated the fact that people were like babies to their electronic devices. The firm fought for market share before going kaput.

Despite the tackiness of the product, the firm had flown in a PR consultant from Montreal to help us launch it. She had bobbed curly hair, wore dark business suits with short skirts, and walked around munching carrot sticks. Nervous as a rabbit. Like her glamourous name, Emily Vale was a mixture of exuberant heights and cipher-like depths. She strutted around nervously but portentously as if fortune were tottering on the success of her product. At the same time, there was a remoteness, a coldness, that suggested hidden depths. The estrogen mafia was in awe of her. She represented some ideal in themselves, she and her new fun toy, that combined professionalism and pleasure. The way they cooed when Emily arrived with a box of complimentary Nipples and handed out one to each worker, you'd think she'd just given out free vibrators. Even Gerry came down out of his office, onto the floor, to take a look. The Nipples came in different shades of skin – from Ethiopian Ebony to the one that Emily had come up with, Wisconsin White. How obnoxious is that? When did our culture come to the point where it was desirable to celebrate the crass? The table with all the women punching buttons on their devices around it looked like a sex toy party.

I drifted away, as if the table were an island and I was floating out to sea.

Later that week, after the product was launched, I would see it and Emily differently. I would stifle my emotions and bend myself towards what she and the firm wanted. But that night, the night of the launch, I was still my own man. Even if I was there at the trendy bar where the Nipple was being launched, manning the projectors and lighted displays, I knew what was going on. I understood the sheer idiocy of the undertaking. I could predict its outcome. I was still my own man.

High-priced martinis and tasteless, grave cocktails. Four projectors flashed up random images and promotional propaganda having to do with the Nipple in the four corners of the bar. No matter where our guests (media, business types, industry insiders, retailers) turned, they would be flashed with electronic trivia about the hunk of plastic we were shilling. Like pimps, we enticed them to squeeze our client's Nipples. I reminded myself that this wasn't going to be my career forever, that our family needed all the money it could get, especially if my ill-fated father was going to try to smuggle himself into the country once more.

It takes a lot of money to smuggle a person into a desirable Western country. Thousands and thousands of dollars. There are no guarantees. When Roshan and I left with our mother, Appa's parents were able to pay using all the savings from their years of running a store. But there was no money left for Appa. He would have to wait before he could approach smugglers outside of Colombo, not from our part of the country, to take him aboard. They got him to somewhere on the East Coast of Africa, but then, he was stuck there for a long time. What choice did he have? Eventually, he chose to go back to Sri Lanka and help his parents rebuild their store. It never returned to its former prosperity and was always in danger of vandalism and looting. My mother heard complaints aplenty; she hardly dared complain about the life she had. After being back for a few months, Appa chose to find the smugglers and get his money back. They pounded him and cracked his head, left him with a concussion. I suppose he was lucky they didn't cripple him or worse. But that was the business. That was the way things were in that country torn by war. No securities, no bonds, no receipts. Some just take your money and run – you never hear from them again.

I was thinking about these things when Doris called out to me: "Thambi, come over here!" Doris is the supervisor on this project. She was twice Emily's age but I respected and even adored her. I got up from the bar and went over. My white shirt and striped tie glowed garishly under the bar's ultraviolet light. Doris and the other women's white teeth stared up at me, crocodiles circling underneath the waterline of their camaraderie. They'd had a few to drink and played cards for nickels and dimes. Out of drunken kindness and belligerence over the evening, they'd invited me to play.

"Thambi, why don't you ever join us?" asked Cynthia.

"Because he doesn't want to be humiliated by a bunch of women." That was Kellisa. Snicker snicker. They think they're so funny, but they have no wit at all. All that remains between their prissy herdlike outsides and what's so ugly and obnoxious on the inside is a few cosmopolitans. My blood was always ready to boil then, with a great deal of angst swirling in it, and I wasn't prepared to like them if they didn't like me.

"Thambi, go pick up some food."

"Yes, Thambi, go do something useful."

A big laugh followed by a few trickles.

"That's not part of my job description," I said.

"Hey, who's in charge here? Doris, Thambi thinks he's in charge."

Emily moved out of the darkness, nibbling on a carrot stick. She was proud yet awkward, tight-fitted, in her skirt and grey blazer. "Come on – I'll go with you," she said and patted my shoulder.

"Krispy Kreme!" shouted Kellisa, pregnant and giggling.

I looked at Emily, who seemed to sense my frustration. It had been a high-profile night for her and her lipstick had been smudged by her sweat from the heat of the table lamps. It looked like her friendly smile had begun to travel, leave her lips to escape down her neck and to her blouse.

"Thambi'll take you. Here –", Doris tossed me her keys. "Cynthia, will you please pick up?"

Emily threw her carrot stick away as if it had been a cigarette and we walked out to the parking lot. In the moonlight, she looked quite svelte, quite attractive. Her face, to me, had always resembled a vase. It had that pleasant elegant symmetry, the only thing marring her Grecian looks being her bobbed curly hair. She liked grey blazers that barely restrained her brown curls, which corkscrewed from her head like a fount of frothy thoughts. They jiggled with her excitement, her pride, from an evening gone well. Her enthusiasm for her job was admirable, even if her product wasn't. The fact that she bit on carrots constantly only seemed to draw more attention to that reddish-brown hair.

"Why don't you like them?" she asked.

"The question is 'why don't they like me?' I like to read. I'm a thoughtful, capable conversationalist."

"That may be so," she said, "but that's not what comes across."

"Oh yeah? What comes across?"

"That you've got an edge. There's something hard about you. Unlikeable."

We got to Doris' white station wagon. I looked at her but she indicated that I should drive, so I got the engine running and the lights on. There was a photo of Doris with her two kids, a boy and a girl, strapped to her sun shield. I looked at the towheaded kids and suddenly Doris didn't seem so bad.

"I just don't like when she allows them to be that way when Gerry's not around," I said.

"They're just nervous around you," said Emily, "Threatened. They're used to guys doing one of two things to them, and you don't do either."

"Hitting on them or ordering them around?"

"Exactly. Watch that car."

We were on the road now, and had turned onto Lakeshore, the way to the all-nite grocery mart.

"You're not nervous around me?" I asked hesitantly, turning to look at her.

The lights from other vehicles highlighted that Grecian urn of a profile, the upturned nose, the bow-like lips. She crossed her arms and said, "No. Why should I be? If anything, I think I understand you."

"I doubt it," I muttered.

"You're a person without a family, without a country. Everywhere you go, you're lost, even your friends are strangers."

When I said nothing, just kept driving, she continued, "Don't be offended. I know what it's like. You only have one parent, right? Was it a divorce?"

"I wish. We're Tamil," I replied.

"What does that mean?"

"That means people are married for life, like a salmon to its spawning ground, like a priest to his God. I just haven't seen my father since I was three. My earliest memories are of me and my mother alone."

"That's rough. Still, you can't beat commitment." She eyed me strangely as we pulled into the parking lot of the box store. The vast expanse of the parking lot in the dark, lit only by the rain of the fluorescent lamplight, made me feel lonely. The woman beside me seemed like a ghost from another world.

"I don't want you to feel down tonight," she said, pressing my hand. "This has been the most important night of my career. Come on, let's go celebrate. Get some food."

I grabbed a cart and pushed it through the doors. She floated beside me, still riding her cloud of success, the sprightly business suit gliding beneath that mop of curly hair. We picked food that we thought the women would like and put it in the cart. We were like somnambulists who thought we were at home. Almost everybody else there was alone – we were the only couple.

"My father's finally coming over in a month," I said. I crossed my fingers in front of her. "I hope."

The other shades moved around us, picking their apples and bagging their pies.

"Kiss me," she said, turning around and grabbing my chin with her hand.

"What?"

"Kiss me – I'm so giddy I feel reckless."

"You're drunk." I pulled free.

"What if I am?"

"I'd rather you wanted me to and meant it."

"Just because I'm drunk doesn't mean I don't mean it," she said. "It just makes it a little easier to say...oh, forget it." She walked away with a nod of her head and I trailed my cart behind her, trying to puzzle out what she wanted me to do.

She walked ahead, fast, padded shoulders firmly squared, not quite allowing me to catch up. What was I scared of? The brush with the moment had been swift and close. I thought of my mother answering that call from the girl in high school, Amma whacking the receiver against the cradle. The phone was still at home somewhere in a box, its shell cracked. Soon I felt the familiar guilt; slightly sick in my stomach, a bitter taste like an alkaline battery rising to my throat. Tamil mothers wield their hypodermics of guilt, their psychological shears, throughout life. The guilt hums through wires emanating from their brains, zapping into our stomachs. Red for guilt, blue for obligation. Why did I feel guilt? Had I not passed the test? I imagined my father in my situation at my age, could not imagine him being so foolish. Here he was now, returning like some old terrible patriarch from Greek mythology, coming back into our lives. How would he and my mother act? I could see the epic struggles that would be visited on our household. The knives and forks clattering with electricity, jumping and dancing to the gales of their argument.

Already, in the cart, there were Twinkies, Jos Louis, cashews and almonds, marshmallows, and olives. What, were they all pregnant all of a sudden? Emily wandered back to me suddenly and dropped a blue pack of Kotex into the cart.

I was dazed and more than a little mortified. What did she mean by this? A waterfall of blood raged its torrential downpour in my mind. Why on Earth was she picking up maxi pads at this time? Was she billing them to our firm? Their being there was not a good thing. But if I picked them up and asked her about them...well, I saw her laughing at me and could not imagine a more foolish position to put myself in. I did not say anything; I continued to the checkout line as if the pads were not there.

A sad pallid cashier checked us through. "Does your girlfriend want this in the same bag with all the other stuff?" She held up the blue package for all the world to see.

"She's not my girlfriend."

"What?"

"She's not my girlfriend and I don't know what to do with those."

"Don't you want them, honey?" asked the cashier, looking at Emily.

"Uh, no." She took out her corporate credit card. "I thought they were on sale but I guess it was the bigger size."

"Neither of them are on sale," said the cashier, looking at us blankly.

"You did that just to embarrass me," I said outside, as we loaded the food into the car.

"You should have seen the look on your face!"

5

When I went into work the following Monday, I felt depressed and lost. I took the subway into the downtown core, thinking about how much I hated my job and the people who worked there. There was no real right for me to feel this way; it wasn't their fault if they preferred the *Sisterhood of the Traveling Pants* to making me feel welcome. Today, they were holding a shower and an extended lunch for Kellisa, who would go on maternity leave soon. Doris had asked me in a token manner a week ago if I wanted to contribute to the fund for it and I had declined; I'd long since stopped pretending to take an interest in their affairs. I serve people as they serve me.

I didn't know if Emily was going and it wasn't her fault if she was. I had no more claim on her than a stranger. Besides, the girl could be so different from one moment to the next – unexpectedly nice, then frustratingly removed. But aren't all women like that? I had been thinking about her on and off all Sunday and the aftertaste of those thoughts came up in my dreams, ascending from my stomach and coating my tongue with an acidic taste as I woke up.

My shift started late in the morning and I got to my desk to find a couple of memos and a small gray envelope. Inside the envelope was Emily's business card with a note stapled to it. The note, in her decidedly neat black script with tall l's that swayed like masts, said: *I'm sorry about what happened the other night. I don't usually act like that – I meant no harm. I was just having some fun and I should have thought better of it. It felt as if we were familiar – like I could have fun with you? I hope there are no hard feelings? Everybody else will be going out to lunch for the shower – even Gerry – I got here too late to pay in. Maybe you'd want to have lunch with me?*

I replaced the card and note inside the envelope and threw it all into the garbage, followed by the memos after I had read them. Her note made me nervous. Then I thought about whether someone might find the envelope, fished it out of the garbage, and ripped up the whole thing into tiny pieces. *Fuck that*, I thought, *do you know how many question marks you used in that message?* Logging onto my computer, I checked my e-mails: there were a few routine things I had to do on our network. I helped people with things that were running slow or had glitches. Lately, because I was so good at my job and there wasn't much to do, I had been given the task of responding to routine e-mails from customers. No big picture stuff, just small things that I sent prepared replies to in response. There was a thank you from the Nipple people for the launch, with a link to their website. I clicked on the link and looked for any information on Emily. I didn't have to look very far because there was something about her on the homepage with a well-taken photograph of her, smiling. She wore a green blazer and her brown mop of hair.

The Nipple and the supporters of TheNipple.com would like to invite Emily Vale to our team for the next two months. Emily is an image and design consultant from Montreal and has made Toronto her new home while the Nipplework is launched. She has implemented successful branding projects with the likes of Midnite Fix Drug Marts and DaisyDukes Lingerie. Her youthfulness and dynamism will make the Nipple a key player in the world of PDA devices in the North American market. We are very pleased to have her on board through the launch of The Nipple and its various skins. Besides consulting, she is also an avid scrabble player and skier.

What the hell was that? I should feel nervous around this phony? I closed the window and got down to my other tasks. My real, inconsequential, time-wasting, meaningless work. Still, I couldn't get the message on her note out of my mind. The bits and pieces of ripped shreds swirled around as if flushed into a toilet basin that wouldn't empty – all those 'I's floating around like the flotsam and jetsam of a shipwreck.

Around lunch, I was making good progress on the day's assignments. I had only checked the scoreboard of my favourite sports website twice, and I was kneading my shoulders, which were stiff, trying to reach back as best as I could.

"What's up, doc?" A low voice crept up behind me and caught me unawares.

"You gone to lunch yet?" Emily stood there in her blazer and pinstripe shirt, the l's in 'lunch' swaying like masts, chewing on a carrot stick. "It's just you and me. You want to grab something to eat?"

With chicken shawarmas in our hands, trying not to get tzatziki sauce everywhere, we sat inside a Lebanese place on

Richmond. She had offered to pay for the sandwiches, which was a nice gesture. But when we got through the line, the cashier, a young tanned Lebanese guy, flirted with Emily. She flirted back. In the end, he gave us our sandwiches for free.

"What's wrong with you now?" she asked as we ate, not looking at one another.

"Did you have to flirt so obviously with that guy? I would have been happy to pay for the food."

"You didn't need to pay."

"You didn't need to flirt. He's a moron and you're an idiot for going along with it. Don't you feel ashamed?"

"If you don't want yours, nobody's forcing you to eat it," she said, putting her foot down. "So what if he gave me the food free? Where's the harm in it? You have to live sometimes."

I couldn't eat the food. It tasted acidic, like lime extract, like dreams I had been wrenched awake from. I didn't even understand why she had this influence on people the way she did. She was thin like a spike or a railroad tie that carried all the magic and physics of enchanted iron. There was a lodestone quality that attracted me yet at the same time roused my anger. Others felt it too. This woman who was not beautiful but pulled you in with her sharp magnetic lines. She was a golf tee whose body, surprisingly, supported a small vase instead of a ball. That elegant, fair face and all that reddish brown hair. I could feel the detente that she had offered me at work. Making an alliance was a much more desirable prospect than showing my indignation. Yet I felt awful. I looked at the cashier who had managed a more successful interaction with Emily than me. However briefly, both had gotten what they wanted. He had pipes that were as big as my head. His head sprouted a strange buzzcut like magnetic filings – both he and I turned towards Emily. He was funny looking but he had done something to improve his physique. My body was formless, growing soft, my head unattractively round as a soccer ball that everybody ended up kicking.

I wanted to push her food off the table and leave. Instead, I pushed away my own tray with the sandwich and condiments spilling out all over the plastic and off the table, creating a clatter as everything fell to the ground. I didn't want the 'free' food and the stupid cashier could clean it up. Emily looked up at me, stunned, and I could feel everybody else in the place freeze, watching us and trying not to seem like they were watching. I had to slide out of there. I realized then that, to everyone else, it must have looked like we had just fought. Perhaps we had. I got out of my seat. A smile began to cross Emily's lips. Never taking her eyes off me, she pushed her own tray off the table and it fell to the floor with an even larger crash, the backs of the trays lying over each other like unmade bedsheets, overlapping their edges. Food was everywhere; the tzatziki and the garlic sauce had flown up and splashed her skirt and my khakis.

"What the hell?" the cashier yelled – he had come around from behind the counter.

I threw a ten dollar bill on the table and we ran out of there.

Our aborted lunch meant that we got back to work before everybody else. We were still hungry. We spent a few minutes going through cupboards, boxes and even other people's desks looking for something to eat. Emily was looking at the photo of Doris's family on Doris's desk when I pulled the photo out of her hand. Placing it back on Doris's desk clumsily and taking Emily's wrist, I pushed her against the grey cubicle divider and kissed her.

"You're trouble," I said. "You bring chaos in your wake."

"I hate chaos," she replied, firmly grasping my soccer ball head in her hands. She made as if to blow into my mouth. I put my other hand against her belly and pushed her into the soft wool of the divider, grinding my hips up into hers ever so slightly, feeling the warmth cross between my churning belly into hers, between our clothes. I let her kiss me but had to strain my neck to keep myself still. She wouldn't kiss me straight. She drew away and then kissed me again. She pulled away and then pulled together, wetting her lips with mine, not staying long enough to make the kisses deep. The faint taste of tzatziki and tahini sauces on her lips. Her face and skin smelled of olives. As if by kissing me and drawing away, she set the pattern for our whole relationship – she pulled away and then pulled back. I moved my hand down between her legs.

"Not yet," she replied and pushed it away. She arched her neck back and I kissed her below the jaw where I could see her veins pulsing between her mouth and heart. I nibbled the flesh and she moaned and pulled me closer towards her violently; we jerked awkwardly against the cubicle divider and sent it sprawling backwards. We tumbled over it and fell on top of each other and the divider, Emily hurting her back and I twisting my foot. Who knew that the cubicle dividers had such weak legs?

We looked about us clumsily. Today was the day for sending things hurtling down. We had to recover ourselves and straighten ourselves out and ignore the minor bruising to put everything back in order before Doris and the others got back from the shower.

6

There went the afternoon. For the rest of the day, I could hardly concentrate on work. I typed listless e-mails to clients about one minor thing after another – and stared right through the cubicle dividers separating me from Emily. My x-rays bored through the dividers, file folders, through other people, through her clothes, her hair, smell, underwear, through her skin itself to her brain, her pulsating heart. Conscious of my feelings, I avoided her for the rest of the day. I must not make too much of it, I said to myself. I hoped she would wait for me after work. Of course I could have texted her but I had ripped up her business card to shreds. Did I really want to be that guy – the person who fished them out of the garbage can and spent his whole afternoon taping them back together?

The sounds of the office wound down. Printers no longer whirred. Paper no longer grated. Chatter ceased and stopped. I wrapped up the files on my desk. Not as much done as I would have liked, but how could I – with half my brain somewhere else? I had started late and I had to finish late but I was aching to get out of there. Packing my bag and leaving, I saw that Emily's desk lamp was still on and it sent a nervous flutter through my stomach. She was still here. But she had not spoken to me all afternoon. I had not contacted her either. She was sitting at her desk when I got round the divider. She swivelled back and forth in her chair, holding a pen between her hands. The pinstripes over her breasts moved up and down as she breathed.

"Hi. How are you?" I didn't know what else to say.

"I didn't get a lick of work done."

"That makes two of us," I replied. I sat down on the edge of her desk and tried to move in for a kiss but she launched herself backwards, scooted her chair out of the way.

"Not so fast."

"Why – what's wrong?" I asked. Was I moving too fast? I still remembered our lunch – the taste of tzatziki and hummus on her lips as I kissed her. That faint smell of olives which arose from her face and hair.

"Are you going to make a complaint about me?" I asked after she didn't reply. "If you are, I have a right to know."

Emily smiled and covered the bottom half of her face. She couldn't look me in the eye. I didn't know what there was to laugh at. She had left me dangling and I didn't know who I was. I was surprisingly forward one moment and insecure the next.

"I can't go out with you." She pointed her pen at me. "The women here would never forgive me."

"How do you know? Have you taken a poll?"

"I know." She stared back at me defiantly.

"Who says we have to go out?" I asked. "Who says they have to know?"

She eyed me curiously. "What are you suggesting?"

"We could meet in private. No one at work would ever have to know." Was this me talking?

"Do you know what that entails? We'd have to pretend, when we're at work, that we hardly know each other. You don't seem the type to restrain yourself. You don't seem the type for an affair."

I riffled some papers on her desk, pushing them around. "Oh, what does it matter what we call it?" I said. "It's what we do with each other that counts."

"This job and this account are important to me," she said, standing up, "and I'm not letting them go for anybody."

"I can understand that."

"I'm warning you. If you screw up anything for me at work, so help me God..."

"I won't," I promised.

I saw an opening and pushed ahead. "Is the sky going to fall on our heads if we go out to dinner just once?"

She walked over and put her arms around my neck. "You may take me to dinner," she said. She leaned in to return my kiss from earlier.

I couldn't take her to dinner that night. I had promised Amma I'd help her with the wedding invitations and I was expected home. So I reluctantly said goodbye to Emily, she gave me a couple of lingering kisses, and I took the subway all the way back to Scarborough.

Wedding preparations were underway. Amma sat in front of two gilded invitations. One was large and fancy and pink with gold ornate lettering. The other was more elegant, blue with raised silver lettering. Both were on beautiful card stock, awaiting our mother's inspection. The pink card was traditionally Tamil, featuring Rama and Sita in the forest, banished yet sitting austerely, content with each other. A deer frolicked nearby. How had our mythology held together so long, even here? The other invitation bore no picture, but its size, and its sophistication, proclaimed assurance and pride.

"Which one do you think we should go with?" asked my mother, pushing the cards around on the table. I knew it was a test.

"The pink one, of course. It's traditional."

"Of course. Lakshmi wants the blue one. She says that the other one is too big – too old-fashioned. She used those words. What's the matter with children these days?"

"So what's the problem?" I asked, knowing full well what the problem was.

"The problem is your brother. That girl has him whipped. He sides with her instead of his own family. Like we're nothing to him – dead and gone."

"Amma, don't be dramatic. You know he doesn't feel that way. Think how stressed he must be – the wedding only two months from now. Where is he anyway – the blushing groom?"

"Hiding in your room. Says he has a headache, doesn't want to talk to me, *hahn*. Let's hope somebody gives him a spine as a wedding present."

"Amma!"

She took my hand and squeezed it. "How was your day, *machan*? Have some food, eat something. Change out of those clothes and have a wash."

I complied with the first part of her request and sat down with some of the rice and curries that lay warm on the stove. It's amazing how different my life was once I walked through our door. How obedient and deferential I became. Here was the Thambi who walked on eggshells around his mother. If the wedding invitation depicted us instead of Rama and Sita, it would portray Roshan crouched in fear, my mother standing and shouting over him, and myself with my hand pressed to my head, enduring a migraine.

My mother vetted a list and ran some names by me. "Should we invite the Ramlanathans?"

"They invited us to their cousins' wedding," I reminded her. This was just a formality – a way of talking with me – in truth, everybody was not only invited but expected to come. Woe betide the person who dared stay away without a good excuse.

"Oh yes, my memory's getting weaker," the great dramatist said. "That's what happens when you get old. Where shall we sit them?"

"Sit them in the back with the Ranganathans. Who knows if they'll come. And you know you're not old."

"Such a son!" She pinched my cheek and I grimaced. "When are we going to get you married?"

"What's the hurry? You'll need me around, now that you're getting older."

She playfully pushed me. "You can marry and look after me as well. I can live with you. If you find a nice girl, she'll remember her duties and be respectful. There'll be no problem. You can't rely on anybody. Only family. Remember that."

"What about Appa?"

Her head flicked. "Appa will be here of course. We'll take care of each other if you don't want us. But old people need grandchildren to take care of. We need something to do."

"Yes, yes, I know all that," I said, "but that's not what I'm talking about. I've heard you two on the phone. Is everything going to work out, or is it going to be a mess? Tell me frankly. He's not going to get in, is he? Do you think he'll screw up?"

She put the invitation list down and looked up. "He's your father! Don't talk about him like that. Of course he's getting through – don't go casting your famous stones all over the place." She softened. "Of course we must think positively. Your brother has gone ahead and acted rashly, without talking to us, that's true. Not that I'm not happy. Of course I am. But I would have liked to have known. Does nobody tell me anything anymore?"

"They meant it as a surprise for you."

"You mean SHE meant it as a surprise. And she got it too. Still and all, we must be grateful. They have money and we have none. That is the way these things go. Roshan is either too cowed or too impulsive. Always so eager to please. Like your father."

"It's a good thing I got your sense then," I said.

She looked at me sadly. "Even you tell me less and less these days. Where is it you go at nights?"

"To the ball games. Basketball."

"See. You don't tell me."

She began looking at the invitation list again. "Still, you *were* the one to get my good sense. Don't go losing it."

"I won't, ma." I got up to wash my plate. I could feel her eyes looking straight into my back, drilling between my shoulder blades.

"Do you think he's going to make it, Amma? What happens next? Is he going to throw everything in order or mess it up even further?"

"God willing, he'll arrive. Papers and passports are being constructed for him. If this doesn't work, these fools aren't going to get their money back. God knows what it will do to that man's confidence."

I walked down the hall to the room that Roshan and I shared. The light bulb had burned out in the hall. The light from the kitchen threw a darkling glare on the old wallpaper. My shadow lengthened and then blended into the darkness. The smell of incense sticks and burnt oil hung in the air and clung to the shadows, baseboards, and wall.

Despite my mother's injunctions, I turned on the bedroom light and woke Roshan up. There he was, a formless lump underneath the covers like a fat caterpillar that had gone into his cocoon, waiting to emerge as a married butterfly and fly away. Climbing up on the bed, I straddled him and punched him about the shoulders. "Hey! Wake up, why aren't you helping Amma in the kitchen? She can't do everything by herself."

"Leave me alone!" He moaned like a baby. "Why are you such a nuisance? Leave me alone!"

"Not until you explain to me why you aren't helping Amma," I replied. "She's doing everything for you. I'm organizing a...bachelor thing. Why aren't you doing something?"

He sat up and stared at me, bleary eyed. Had he been crying? "I am doing something. I'm getting married."

That's when it sank in. He wasn't doing this only for himself, only to get away...he felt that he was doing this for them. For us? It was a whole new level of twisted. Did he not like Lakshmi anymore? Besides her being a little overweight, wasn't she beautiful to him? She had not had to lift a finger very often in her life, as Roshan and I had. Didn't overweight people find each other attractive? Didn't they look for each other? Or is it weird to them – all that flesh colliding? I didn't know. I had the opposite problem – I looked as drawn out as an Egyptian mummy, as skinny as a beanpole, as withered as a broom, from all my running around.

Roshan searched around for his glasses, found them on the night table, and put them on. He pushed a rough hand through his greasy hair. "I don't know what to say to either of them," he said. "Lakshmi wants to go with the blue ones. Amma's been giving me the cold shoulder all night."

"Make a decision. Help them move forward," I replied, searching his eyes.

"I can't – don't you see? I cast my vote in either camp and immediately the other one pounces on me. I can't win."

"You manage a small team at work," I said, "you make hundreds of decisions a month."

"This is different," he managed to wheeze, lifting up his arms and grasping his head.

"So you're just going with what Lakshmi tells you? Don't you know what this is doing to Amma?"

"No, I don't! You're the one she likes! You're the one she trusts! So go talk to her, console her. You two can spend all your time with each other now that I'm gone."

"Don't think you're special just because you're getting married."

For a second, a sulphurous flare sizzled and went off inside his eyes. Like the smell of cordite in the air. He pushed me off the bed. I banged my head and shoulders against the baseboards. I was on the bed and then I was on the floor.

I got up and rubbed my head. Roshan was already back to his old self, solicitous and wet. He was sorry and tried to help me off the floor.

"I don't think anything's really hurt," I said, and rubbed my head again. It smarted.

I climbed into my bed, five feet away from Roshan, and slid underneath the covers, still in my clothes. I watched him, sitting up, his arms around his knees. He was sorry, and the usual feeling between us, the usual amount of worry, returned.

"How's work?" he asked.

"The usual," I replied. "Same stupid old people."

"That's because you always go for these dead-end contract jobs. You go from contract to contract." I imagined him smoking a cigarette in his undershirt, like some clichéd private investigator. I imagined him talking like a duck. "You never settle down. You never do anything serious. Just push with the least amount of effort."

The old feeling had settled between us; the usual routine. I sang *Everything I do, I do it for you* by Bryan Adams to annoy him. After a few bars, he still had not said anything.

"Roshan, everything's going to be alright, isn't it?" I asked him the same question I had asked Amma.

"I don't know... I don't know," he replied after a pause. "It's all happening too fast."

7

She was a hard nut to crack, my Emily. She didn't want to go to a restaurant after all and this disappointed me. I had had the vision of us dressed to the nines, sailing out the door. It would have given me pleasure to spend my money on her instead of saving, saving, saving for rainy days. Enough with the rainy days – it was time to enjoy some sunshine when we could. She insisted that we buy some groceries and take them back to her place. I did not have her calm, deliberate voice and so did not have a comeback as to why we should go out. Nor did I have her detachment and amiability toward everything we did. It was as if Roshan had taken the fill of these qualities from our parents and I was left with the rest, uncertainty and a biting discontent. I secretly wished that I could be like my mom, resilient and resourceful, but it was circumstances that had made her this way. I had not yet been confronted with the circumstances that would define me.

I thought of Amma as Emily sat in front of me at her dining table, finishing the last of the goat's cheese and vegetables and wine we had picked up. A salad bowl with flakes of lettuce, more of the goat's cheese, the sticky smell of vinaigrette and olive oil and green olives stuffed with pimentos circling its rim sat between us. Always, the smell of olives circled her. As if she had been born in an olive grove, ripening on the vine, waiting to be plucked. Amma's face, as hard as a walnut, her view of life just as hard, paled beside Emily. I knew my features were strained and withered like my mother's. My own body, like a balloon floating along on an uncertain string, paled beside Emily.

She wore almost all black. Her sweater was soft like a second skin, so it gave me pleasure to touch it. She stood out against her apartment, which was painted in a golden amber hue. It was an unlikely colour and an unlikely apartment in a decrepit neighbourhood that smelled of trash rotting in the alleyways. I had nothing against the indigent parts of town, but I could not reconcile this place – the speckled walls that shimmered yellow in the candlelight – and the mound of boards and beer empties outside her fire escape. Her curly auburn hair, reflected by the carrot sticks she always snacked on, stood out from the calligraphy of her body.

Oh, she was calligraphy and I was Caligula! My conversation, like bad spices liberally seasoned on rotting meat, covered my rotting desires. She talked about her apartment. "It's not Montreal but I like it. It has a fire escape and I need that."

"What do you need to escape from?" I asked.

"Nothing – no, I mean to be able to look out on to the street without having to lock up. All the apartments in Montreal have such lovely steep metal staircases but it's hell trying to move in and out of them. I had the walls painted as soon as I got here. All the apartments in Montreal are painted such warm colours. Makes you want to have people over."

"How long will you be here?" I asked.

"A long time I hope." She paused in her nibbling of her carrot stick and waved it in the air above us for an answer. "I'll have to do some travelling to promote the Nipple. If things go well, they'll put me on another contract here."

"You'd like that?"

"I think so. You don't like the Nipple, do you?"

I leaned away but I didn't think it was wise to lie. "It's tacky. It's crass, like the women at work. The ON button is a nipple itself, it's a huge dilated aureole."

"It makes you uncomfortable."

"I didn't say that. What's the point in it – that's all. Do we need to go here as a society?"

"What's the harm in it?" she asked, eyeing me closely. "It makes money and it's fun. That's all. That's why the girls at work like it."

"That doesn't necessarily make it good."

"Just because you think something is good doesn't make it so."

We came to a stop. The tension was frustrating. She saw my eyes wander over the V neck of her sweater and plunge down her cleavage. I wanted to take her face in my hands.

She cleared her throat and leaned back, took another carrot stick. "What excuse did you give your mother?" she asked.

"I told her that I was going to a Leafs game."

"She bought it?"

"I think so."

"Who are they playing tonight?"

"The Penguins."

"So that means you can't sleep over?"

I shook my head.

"Then we'd better get to it, no?"

She allowed me to pick her up and carry her to the bedroom. Light as a feather from Cupid's wing. Like Cupid and Psyche, I had to undress in the dark until she found some matches and a scented candle which she placed in a bowl and lit. Except, she was the God and I was the mortal. I felt like an immigrant in the land of desire and that I should not be there. I should not see that sweater come off, the angular shoulder blades glint in the soft light. The belly that undulated like a soft wave of sand. She was a streak of oil in the water. So noiselessly did she shimmer out of her clothing and come to me.

Her arms around my naked shoulders, the smell of her hair in my nostrils. My hands on her waist, we circled and rocked slowly around the room. We did not speak and it was the first time that I felt I made true contact with her. Her guard came down and I felt how slender was the thing that had come up the river from Montreal, into my life. I lifted her to the bed, she almost perching on my forearm like a bird upon a tree.

The flickering light and the smell of candle wax made me aware that the room was burnt yellow like the others. She had a couple of unframed posters on the wall. One of that famous Banksy print with the handkerchiefed guy throwing a bouquet of flowers. The other one of Picasso's Guernica. They were arranged so that it looked as if Banksy's protester had just thrown something that had landed in Picasso's picture. In the flickering light, it was as if the Molotov kick had just shattered the whole room and it was going to pieces. The walls were made of speckled pieces of sand that swirled in some eddying vortex.

I went to work and sank into that sand.

Later, we were sweating, warm and rubbery, our bodies around each other. She held me with her legs and pulled me towards her. I fumbled with a condom, the most unromantic act possible at that moment, while her foot played with my back. It had been a long time since the last time I had a woman in my arms and I was all nerves. It was as if my whole body was erect, tense and engorged. It didn't know if I was happy or pained. More pained. Finally, I had the condom on and she pulled me to her with her legs and wrapped them around my waist.

I guided myself towards her but couldn't find my place. I took time to stroke her thighs and find her with my fingers to guide myself in again. I couldn't do it. Was I shrinking? No – if anything, the erection was tight as a drum, most painful. I could barely pass myself into her. Something seemed wrong with the angles at which we'd been created. I tried adjusting our positions, placing pillows underneath her and then even underneath myself. Nothing worked and I felt as constricted as a clenched fist down there, any more discomfort and I was sure I'd be pissing blood. I thought of the package of Kotex she had picked up at the supermarket.

What stronger sign than this could there be? As if a god had designed us to be incompatible – we did not fit.

Emily stroked me on the shoulder and sat up. "It's alright," she said, "go to the fridge and get me a carrot."

"You're feeling hungry?" I said in disbelief.

"That's not what I meant," she replied, "I have a big bag of carrots in the fridge. Go get me one, as smooth as possible, not too crooked, and without a sharp end."

I did as she asked and turned on the light. Her stark nakedness sobered me up and I finally shrank. I couldn't look at her thighs or breasts, I couldn't even look at her shoulders. My eyes turned downwards, travelled down her legs. At the bottom of her right leg, around the ankle of that cool slender tentacle, was a red and black tattoo – a stylized eye with sun rays shooting from it. It was only later that I learned that this was the Eye of Horus and Emily had gotten it in a fit of pique in her younger Montreal days. The Eye seemed to sense my discomfiture and winked at me.

"Hurry and come back to me," urged Emily.

I did as she said, found a carrot, and came back. She had turned off the light and blown out the candle and I could only just make her out. Emily felt the carrot in the dark, seemed to approve, and stroked me on my shoulders and chest to soothe me, calm me down. She placed a lingering kiss on my belly. Then she asked me for a condom. I passed her the prophylactic and she slipped it deftly over the carrot, unrolling it so that it completely covered the shaft. "I'll pull you off afterwards," she said, "but first use this."

She handed it to me. It was like a cudgel draped in a polyurethane sock. I used it gingerly, poking it inside her like I was looking for something underneath the sink.

"Deeper," she commented.

I pushed deeper, feeling some of her spasms of pleasure ride up the carrot and through my arm. I never felt comfortable pushing very hard for fear that I would hurt her but she abandoned herself to it and we somehow found her rhythm. This way I was able to lie alongside her and kiss her, suck on her hair and brush my lips under the heft of her breasts. She finally began to climax and somehow, just by rubbing myself against her legs, I came too. I spilled over her thighs, belly and sheets as if I hadn't been released for weeks. I could feel it sliding and dripping off my thighs, onto her sheets.

Afterwards, she took the carrot away and pulled the condom off. She pretended to bite into the carrot and made as if to eat it. "What's up doc?" she asked. Can you believe that? "What's up doc?"

8

At home, nerves were aflutter about the pending arrival of my father. Our ganglia hummed and buzzed to the time his flight would arrive, three days from now. Meanwhile, preparations for the wedding continued. Neither Lakshmi's parents nor ours had wanted a long engagement and so Roshan and Lakshmi were due to be married in the dead of winter. The wedding was to take place on December 15th, barely a month away, and there were a million things to be done. The invitations were finally printed and sent out. My mother and Lakshmi had come to an agreement. They settled for blue, which my mother hated, and a size that Lakshmi felt was too improbable. The invitations were large and it was as if my mother was shouting by sending them out. With gilt lettering on high quality stock and with illustrations of Krishna and Radha (instead of Rama and Sita) dancing in the forest, she shouted out from the rooftops: my eldest is getting married! Though we did not have means, we lavished every last penny on the preparations. A hall was rented and a DJ hired. Bangles and saris were bought. Our apartment was festooned with streamers and garlands. We went to a priest to consult him about the ceremonies, to one person, then another to discuss this and that, payments and fees.

The priest, naked from the waist up with his sacred thread, though he had long hair and sacred ash on his forehead, was a modern man who constantly talked on his cellphone. Like a realtor, he was always on some unending call to a mysterious client or answering an urgent plea from someone else. "Yes, of course we can do it, but you must listen to me...don't worry. These things will happen... listen, I have to talk to these two...think about what I said." He conducted his business in dribs and drabs while we tried to iron out the details of the wedding. Hindu weddings are gruelling day-long affairs, the order and rituals mystifying to even the most ardent of worshippers. I had seen this priest, soft bellied and long haired like all priests, chanting mantras and overseeing pujas at our local temple. He was bearded and jovial, dismissive to my brother and condescending to me, and I decided that I preferred him and his cellphone at a distance in the temple rather than entwined in our personal affairs.

Roshan and I returned to my mother at home, who, back from the wedding hall, seemed as exhausted as we were. Her pottu, the red dot on her forehead, pulsated like a throbbing vein as she talked.

"I just got off the phone with that man," she said, referring to our father. "He says that everything's set. The flight's on Thursday. He's finally coming!"

"Wonderful news, ma," said Roshan, going to rub her feet dutifully.

"Thambi, make me some tea," said my mother, nodding towards me. This has always been my role and I can now make tea with boiled milk perfectly to suit a Tamil heart's delight. I sort of enjoy this duty. I've always been behind the scenes, making the tea, listening to conversations, ears open, mouth closed. This really was incredible news about my father. We had talked to him a couple of days before in London, England, and he seemed in great spirits. His enthusiasm was contagious and we caught the fever of his arrival, the news like electricity constantly sending our brains buzzing. Money had been transferred, agents had been paid, a fake passport had been constructed, papers had been created, and my father was holed up in some basement in London waiting to ride to Gatwick on Thursday. He had always been ahead of us in time but now the gap was finally closing. Time and space were collapsing. I pushed any doubts I might have had about his arrival to the bottom of my cluttered heart: I willed everything to work out right.

"What do you think about your father coming now?" asked my mother.

"Excited, of course. It's what we've all been waiting for," I replied, careful to balance the cup and saucer, taking care to step around Roshan, who was still bent over, rubbing Amma's feet. She looked down and patted Roshan on the back, returning my gaze as she took the tea from me. I wondered about everything that gaze held.

"It'll be nice to have a father around," said Roshan lightheartedly. Somehow it was the dutiful thing to say but it was also troubling. I got the sense again that it was him and our father against us. His voice came up as if out of the ground, from underneath that bent back of his. "It's strange to meet someone that you've only talked to on the phone for the last so many years," he said.

"Well, if it's strange for you, imagine what it must be like for me," said my mother between sips. "I've gotten so used to doing everything myself. I just imagine that man running around like he was twenty-five. He has to learn to take it easy on his heart and slow down. He feels that he's always right. I don't know how he's going to handle living here. It's not like it is back home."

"He's not going to understand that these days, the women run everything," I said.

"They always did," said my mother, taking a long drink from her cup.

"That reminds me – has Lakshmi talked to you about our shervanis?" I asked.

"Didn't you hear? She came over here," said my mother, laughing. "She stormed over here and yelled at him. As frustrating as that girl can be, you have to admire her wilfulness. She gets things done."

"Hmmmph," Roshan muttered, picking himself off the floor. He walked to our room. I couldn't see his face.

"Don't mind him," said my mother, draining her cup meditatively. "The fact that your father's coming back is in no small part because of Lakshmi and her family. We have to swallow our pride and be nice to her, whatever it takes. I want you to go to the airport this Thursday with us; make sure everything works perfectly. I love Roshan, he's a good son, but you're the one who inherited my good sense...you're the one I depend on."

On Thursday, we all waited at Pearson Terminal Three for my father to come through customs. The first snow of the season fell heavily outside the large glass windows of the airport and it brought a bitter, howling cold with it. The buildings seemed to prop each other up, trying their best to stay open and lit. We were all bundled in padded jackets and large scarves and mittens. The floors were covered in streaks of slush and wet puddles. There were many of us waiting for the passengers of the British Airways flight to come through and we all jostled around each other, anticipating the climactic moment. Lakshmi and Roshan, my mother, and myself. I thought of Emily as we waited, her face, especially her eyes and the faraway look that she sometimes had, as if her irises were shrinking. I saw her whenever I could after work, but our father's arrival meant that I would not be able to see her properly the way I wanted to for a while.

We had quickly developed a routine. As long as the Leafs were doing well and playing home games, I could tell my mother that I was going to a game after work. I proceeded to Emily's apartment and we ate quickly before slipping out of our clothes and burning off the calories. It bothered me that my licence depended upon the fortunes of a team so unfortunate. I would switch to the Argos if necessary. After the snatched time in Emily's apartment, she watched ESPN with me so that I could talk about 'the game' at home. At first, I bought a scalped ticket to a seat in the nosebleeds to cover my alibi, but of course, Amma never asked to see it. I cooked for Emily if she was tired and she massaged my shoulders. We watched movies or parts of them on TV, but always we ended up making love. I had finally relaxed and was able to uncurl myself into her; the carrots stayed inside the fridge. These quiet moments, drowning in her, were especially important to me as they were an escape from the chaos and calamity and confusion back home.

Passengers began to emerge. There was a flurry of movement; overcoats and bags and hugs and feet. Finally, he came through. It was definitely him. Shorter than I imagined, heavier around the face and the eyes, he was the spitting image of Roshan. Save for the generational gap, they could have been brothers. There were lines in his skin everywhere, as if, living on the opposite side of the world, he had lived two years for every one of ours. He looked even older than my mother, and his grey unkempt hair went everywhere, accentuating the bewildered look that he had. It was as if the last twenty years had passed him by, leaving him rooted squarely in the twentieth century, forever wondering what had happened to the world. Nevertheless, the stockish body, the bluffing manner – this was Roshan in another twenty-odd years. Looking around him with a stunned mien, he didn't see us.

We were all silent for a moment, contemplating his appearance and the differences between our expectations and his actual existence. It was as if we were all thinking about what would happen if we didn't call out his name and just turned around as a unit and went home.

"Appa!" called Roshan, and the spell was broken.

He wheeled around with his lone small suitcase and looked at us. For a moment neither party moved. We just stared. As if to oblige, nobody walked between us. Our father was dressed unbelievably in khaki pants, a polo shirt, and a light jacket. As if he was going golfing – in this weather! What was in the suitcase? He came up to us and hugged us awkwardly. First Roshan and then myself, and then he stiffly placed a hand on Lakshmi's shoulder. She tried her hardest not to tremble. Then he finally looked at my mother. This was a moment that they had both anticipated for years.

That Sri Lankan imperiousness took over. They clasped each other only briefly. Our father pulled our mother towards his arms and kissed her on the cheek. She turned towards his chest as if she were a little girl ready to cry and disintegrate into him. So much for my poor walnut of a mother; she was moist as a cake on the inside. Urgently they separated, as if too much emotion had been shown. Both held their hands towards their chests, anxious not to touch. Had they looked at each other the first time this way, before marriage? An agreement that some contract had been fulfilled hung in the air and they said each other's names softly.

I took Appa's lone case while Roshan gave him his own coat and took our father's jacket for himself. To make his ridiculous getup complete, Appa was wearing tennis sneakers. Not even winter boots! It was this one detail that brought home how tenuous his presence really was in our lives. How ramshackle and unprepared everything had been for the old man during the past two weeks, how slight a thing was the hope he flew in upon. Our father collapsed upon Roshan for support. "I feel so tired," he said. "It's been a hell of a three weeks."

Of course, we were dying for him to tell us all about the last three weeks but now was not the time. We asked him if he was hungry but he said no. He wanted to get home, to see where we were living, as soon as possible. We pulled out and I thought of the time after Amma's birthday. This time, my brother drove and Appa occupied the space where Lakshmi had sat, looking in astonishment at everything outside the window. Everything covered in a blanket of white. Appa turned on the heat as high as possible. The first thing we would have to do would be to get him a proper coat. Lakshmi was stuck in the back with us, between my mother and myself, and she bristled. The car felt too full. The ghostly presence of my father had materialized. Memories sped away past us in the car's wake, jet lag and time zones realigning. Time stalled temporarily, even flew backwards.

It did feel astonishing to finally have a father there, in our lives. A man to look up to; Roshan was goodhearted but there was something womanly about him. It felt strange to meet my father, someone I could barely remember, as if for the first time. I vaguely remembered him walking on the beach with me when I was three.

We took him to a shopping mall to buy a proper winter jacket. He was amazed by how much there was of everything: clothes, food, products.

"Can a coat really cost this much?" he asked, turning around a black goose down jacket, and calculating the cost in rupees in his head.

"Don't worry about it – I'll pay for it." I was in awe of him. This grand man like a short, vast elephant, whom I had come from.

"Do you really have that much money?" he asked, spinning, bewildered. "Don't you save your money for other things?"

He criticized me for being extravagant while I just wanted to buy him the best thing I could. That's how fast things can change between two people. After all, come on, is a winter jacket not an important thing? A feeling of tension in the air and nobody to come to my aid. I finally shrugged my shoulders and we went to Zellers, where we found a much less expensive item which he accepted without fanfare. He didn't even see it as a gift; he saw it as his money being spent – all of our money was also his money and he saw no reason to spend it so foolishly. He wore his new coat – a thin pale blue polyester jacket padded with cotton that I knew would wear out soon. I found it ugly. I found him ugly in it. Meanwhile, he wore it with pride.

He still refused to be taken out for food, so the first thing we did was go to Lakshmi's house. I didn't even bother to petition for a purchase of new shoes. I was already learning to anticipate and resent his responses.

Lakshmi lived with her parents in a large house in a new development in Richmond Hill. We had to drive through an increasing blizzard to get north of the 401 and my father hummed and sighed all the way there. His eyes took in the large stone dwelling, in newly modelled salmon-coloured stone with its large windows. I could tell that he was amazed at the sheer size and would inevitably be disappointed with our tiny, cramped apartment when we arrived there a few hours later.

Inside, we were seated in the living room. Lakshmi's father is a small, thin man with a moustache, large glasses, and prone to wearing sleeveless sweaters. Her mother is short and round like a pudding or a turkey and serves both these things to us at Christmas even though she is Hindu just like we are. That evening, her father was wearing a burgundy sweater and her mom wore a white blouse like a brown June Cleaver. Their house was spacious and spotless with large rugs, glass tables, and fake granite counters. On the glass coffee table were dishes of nuts and candy. Lakshmi's mother brought us all tea in bone china cups and saucers.

I sat next to my mother while my father sat by himself. Roshan sat with Lakshmi in a loveseat beside us.

"It's good to finally meet you," said Lakshmi's father, welcoming our father with a warm handshake. "How was your trip over?"

"You couldn't imagine it and I hope you never have to go through something like that," muttered Appa as if he was still cold from the weather outside. "All the waiting and grovelling to other people so that you can survive long enough to make it over."

"Well, he won't have to. I think we've all finally made it," said Lakshmi's mother.

"Yes, and we really appreciate what you've done. All of us," said Amma to them, putting a hand on our father's shoulder.

"What do you mean?" asked my father with a bewildered, indignant look that exploded on his face. It was becoming more and more of a permanent feature.

"You mean you don't know?" asked Lakshmi, unable to completely eradicate that hint of delight at our expense.

"Appa..." said Roshan.

"You mean to tell me...," began my father, " No....What do you mean? Roshan?"

"Appa, Lakshmi's part of the family now," said Roshan. "She wanted to help."

He looked around at us as if we had already let him down. Jet lag and disorientation compounded his feelings. I pulled out a smile from the bottom of my fraudulent heart when he looked at me, but I couldn't help its twisting into a smirk.

"You've lied to me. You've all lied to me and you've let these people pay while you prance around offering to buy coats for three hundred dollars. Don't you have any shame?" His glance cut into all of us as he looked around fiercely. Piano wire cut into my stomach. The frustration about the coat came up with it.

To our surprise, it was Lakshmi who stood up. "I'm insulted," she said. "We put out money to bring you over here and you talk as if we're nothing to you. Appa, say something. Don't let this man talk to you like that."

Before her father could say something, our mother cut in, trying to smooth things over. "Manish, Susila, don't get him wrong. He's just –"

But she in turn was cut off by our father: "*Adai!* You will not go against me in front of others."

My mother turned and faced him to look him in the eye, as if to say that was enough. But he was having none of it. "Don't look at me like that!" he shouted.

"Why can't you let me be happy? Just this once?" she asked. Amma held his gaze for a second longer, two seconds, three, then looked down and away. She was defeated and would never challenge him again. The mother I had known for most of my life was gone, just like that. The red pottu on her forehead – the symbol of marriage, the one thing that never changed in her appearance – a large expressive wound.

Lakshmi's parents, dear old Manish and Susila, were horrified. The storm clouds were gathering.

"So who's paying for the wedding?" asked our father in his rage.

"Say something!" I whispered to Roshan.

"We're both paying for the wedding," said Roshan finally. My mother said nothing but just stared. We could see her thoughts as naked as fish bones after the meat and the skin have been gutted. So this is how it's going to be, she thought. The drama has started and he has only been here a couple of hours.

"No!" said my father. "We can pay for the wedding. We can afford to do that. And we'll pay you back for the money you paid the agents. Every single rupee, no matter how long it takes. We're not beggars. Is this how you've been living? We don't need to take anybody's charity!"

But the problem was that we *did* need the help of Lakshmi's family. We couldn't pay for everything on our own – I was sure of it. It's true that Laskhmi's family was trading down by allowing her to marry Roshan, but they seemed like progressive types: well travelled, acquainted with Western culture, slightly more easygoing and indulgent. Lakshmi was their only daughter, their only child. They wanted her to be happy. Roshan had done well in school, was conventional, observed the necessary duties, and was now a junior manager. Once Lakshmi had married, she would never need to work again. The divine purpose behind the place she worked at had been to meet Roshan Navaratnam and now that destiny had been fulfilled. Their horoscopes matched. Manish and Susila were sure of things and everybody understood it. Lakshmi's role had been prescribed long ago. She would settle into family life happily and produce grandchildren that they could dote upon, and they would be able to tell others that she had graduated from university with a Bachelor's, and it would please them to help her out with money. They just wanted her to be happy as she did these things. For some darkly fathomable reason, she seemed happy with Roshan, bossing him around. We all knew where everybody stood until our father arrived. And he sensed none of this.

I felt very uncomfortable there with them, with all of the gloom and the alien heaviness of our father hanging around our necks. I wished I was with Emily, lying with her amongst her blankets, my head cradled in her long arms. The oily smell of her hair and olive hands. How long would it be before I could sneak out and see her again?

9

So we fucked and fucked and fucked. I drowned myself in her to get away from my family. We didn't even bother to eat anymore. It was hard to avoid each other at work so as not to tip anybody off; the charge from the night before still hovered around us, lifting our hair, jumping in magnetic lines from my eyes to her mouth, from her hips to my thighs. When I did bring food over to her place, I ate it off her belly or legs; so engrossed were we in each other and serious about the sex. Less and less often came the times when I could get away from my family. My mother rarely questioned why I was late or where I had been – a leniency I exercised as the privilege of being the younger son. Our father squatted at home like a bullfrog in his seat of power, flicking his tongue out at me and hissing when I didn't come home straight from work. I resented him for it. Once I came home and he was the only one waiting up, sitting on the sofa in the dark, while the others had gone to sleep. It was after two in the morning and I had caught the last subway and bus home. He was in his blue saram and undershirt and looked as if he had dozed off despite his best efforts to stay awake and keep warm the displeasure he had for my activities. Drool had crusted on the top of his undershirt and I loathed to see him like this, waiting to pounce, his hand on his bedraggled head.

"Just where is it that you go to at all hours of the night?" he asked, unfolding his thick legs off the couch and placing his palms squarely on his knees.

"To sports games – I've told you before," I said.

"How many games do you see? And how much money do you spend on them? Why would you rather go to these games than spend time with your own family?"

"What is this?" Amma had woken up and turned on the light in the hallway.

"Tell your son," said my father, "that he is to come home straight after work. That he is to help his family as much as he can. That I am still his father and I'm not afraid to show him what that means." He raised his palm at an angle in a forceful gesture.

"We don't do that here," said my mother.

"Tell your husband," I said, "that I am a grown man. That I treat people as they treat me. And that he is welcome to try me anytime he wishes."

It was the anger speaking of course, my bluff, but my father could not accept what I had said. At our worst times, I could have said something like this to my mother and known that it would be diminished after the heat of the moment, but she too was very far from me at that moment. She had caved in and become someone else to my father.

"I have to sit down or my blood pressure..." he said. "My blood is boiling to see what's happened to you. What do you think I did in Sri Lanka? Why do you think I stayed there? For my own pleasure? Not to go to sports games every night, I can tell you."

"Tell your son that I don't want to have anything more to do with him," said my father. "He obviously has grown too big for his parents. It's all your fault."

My mother looked at him and then looked at me, blinking in the dim light, and already I was starting to feel guilty. "Come, don't take it to heart," she said, "Thambi's always been a little emotional. It's not worth fighting over, so close to the wedding!"

When he didn't speak, she looked at me. "Thambi, don't be like that. Your father doesn't mean it. That's just his way. Come – say you're sorry!"

And then, just to get them off my back, I said "I'm sorry." I continued, after a moment's reflection, "I'm sorry it's come to this. Maybe it's time that I should finally move out. I always thought that I'd stay with you to help you out and save some money but it looks like you don't need my help anymore. I don't need to be questioned every time I go out."

A freshly pained look crossed my mother's face. "If you go, I wouldn't know what to do," she said, thumping my father on his back – this helped bring his blood pressure down. "My heart would break."

It killed me that my mother's artifice was gone, that she said things she truly felt for the first time without coaxing, but the conditions which procured them had been brought on by me. My father slumped as if the fight had gone out of him too. He purposely would not look at me, pointedly showing how much he thought of my worth. Slowly, Amma coaxed him up with her hands and back to bed.

The next night, I was back at Emily's. I lay with my head in her arms, after sex. I told her about the conversation with my parents. She listened without saying anything. My body had gotten used to her. Long gone were the carrots, a great relief to my ego. My body was used to her vase-shaped head, her slender hips, the Eye of Horus at her ankle which winked conspiratorially. We licked each other's bodies dry of sweat and absorbed each other's smell. Even if I had nothing left, we would go at it again, ignoring time, shuddering to dry heaves, ejaculating air. We fucked with force and desperation, as if our secret idyll would be shattered at any moment.

Emily turned on the light and went to the bathroom. The tattoo of the Egyptian eye blinked bright black and red on her right ankle. I only saw it in the light and she was rarely fully naked in the light. Trying to shake myself out of the post-coital daze and anxiety, I looked around. It was hard not to allow my brain to be bludgeoned by the after-feelings of sex, the soft patter of sensuality that hung around when I was with her. Sometimes, if I carried it into work with me the next day, it became melancholy; I hardly got any work done because I missed her apartment; I felt as if everybody could read it off me and I had to hide at my desk. She was not a selfish lover, the first woman I had met who truly was not one, but she was selfish in how much of herself she shared with me. She gave me her body, parcels of her time and attention, but little else. I had grown hungry for more.

I looked around and realized for the first time that there weren't any photos of her family around. Just the speckled sand walls and the prints by Banksy and Picasso. Did she even have any brothers or sisters? I had no idea. We made love, talked about the people at work, watched ESPN, and then I left. We were at the same time both intimate and not.

She came out of the washroom in a bathrobe, which made me hastily reach for my underwear and T-shirt.

"Hey, I just noticed for the first time," I said, "you don't have any photos of your family or anybody else."

"I don't like to clutter my walls with that stuff."

"What are you talking about? You have that huge Picasso print with a bull and all those screaming women. Don't you want something a little warmer to decorate your place with?"

"I don't need pictures to think of my family," she replied irritably. She swatted the air with her palm. "I hate that sentimental stuff."

"What are you talking about?" I asked again. "Who lives like that? Our family only lives in an apartment with one more room than you have, and the walls are packed with photos of friends and relatives. They're in cheap frames, sure, but that's okay – we're not trying to make it into *Architectural Digest*."

"You want to pick a fight?" she asked. "If you do, you can go home. I don't have the patience."

"I'm not fighting...just incredulous. You never talk about your family or really anything outside of work. We have abstract discussions. When are you going back to Montreal?"

"This weekend actually. I have to handle promotion of the Nipple there."

"How long will you be gone?"

"A few days." She came over and sat beside me, taking my chin in her hands. "What's wrong? What's ailing you?"

"It's us." I looked at the beautiful vase-shaped head, its fine nose and evenly set eyes, to see if there was understanding there. "Don't you want more than this? I'm not complaining, but don't you want more?"

"What more could you possibly want? We eat, we make love, we rarely fight, we have a good time."

"There isn't time to fight," I said, shaking my head. "I'm almost thirty and I can't keep it up."

"Then why not get an arranged marriage like your brother? Is that what you want? To cry yourself to sleep like your mother while you hear her through the bedroom walls?"

"No, I wouldn't do that. Don't condescend to me."

"Then what is it that you want?" She shouted, perhaps for the first time.

"I want an arranged relationship instead of an arranged marriage. I want what we have but I want to make it official – I want to go out with your arm on my shoulder. I want to know what I'm coming home to."

"You want to marry?"

"Eventually, yes."

"No, no, no, no...." She stood up and paced around the room, clutched her head. "You don't understand. How long have we known each other? A couple of months – if that. How many women have you been with before me?"

I held up four fingers.

"So I am your fifth," she said. "You can barely make a fist with a finger for each of us. And already you're pummelling yourself with it and saying the word 'marriage'!"

"I don't need to be with anybody else to decide," I said, looking down at the sweaty sheets. I was too ashamed of my desire to look her in the eye. "It's you I want."

"I don't know, I don't know..." she repeated, coming back to bed and taking my hands. "I don't know what this is. You don't know what this is. I knew it was fine and that it worked until now. Now you're ruining it."

When I didn't say anything, she continued. "I've never thought too seriously about marriage. There's something about the contract that doesn't make sense. All that striving and longing for something that creates so much sadness and pain. Does that make sense to you?"

"What else is there? I want to be a part of your life. That's what people do when they see each other."

"You are a part of my life." She was still holding my hands. "You're part of it now. And now is all we really have."

"You don't really believe that."

She pulled her hands away, balling them into fists. "I want to punch you in the mouth to make you shut up. What's wrong with you? You never complained before."

"I was scared of losing you before."

"You can't just change the terms like that. Why are you ruining it?"

"Something's changed between us."

"Just like that? How do you know I feel the same way?" She drew back, dagger eyes pointed in my direction. Those delicate antennae of hers were flitting all over the place. "And what are you going to say to your mother and father? Are you going to invite me over for Sunday dinner? Are you going to take me to the temple?"

"One step at a time," I said.

"Jesus Christ! You'd better get dressed and get out of here. Maybe you'll make more sense when I'm back from Montreal."

"Can I tune into the sports network?"

"No, you'd better go."

My heart full of anxiety, I did as she asked. She whisked herself to the bathroom and stayed there while I finished dressing. The last thing I saw was that black and red Eye of Horus, her ankle flashing beneath her robe as she strode out of the room. Emily stayed in the bathroom the whole time, did not even respond when I said goodbye through the door.

How had I ruined it? What had I done? I walked down the stairs to the sidewalk, spilling with frozen trash and boxes, and made my way home.

10

I did not want to go into work the following week. I did not want to see her face with those dark brown eyes that were forever sinking into the quicksand of her skin, back from Montreal. I did not want to wear my brains at my heels. Amma had to rouse me out of bed and I quickly showered and dressed while she forced food at me which I barely touched, before slinging my bag over my shoulder and rushing out to catch the bus.

A box sat waiting for me at my desk, card in an elegant pearl envelope leaned precariously against it. As before. I had a sense of déjà vu and thought of ripping up the card and throwing the package into the trash. She was trying to get closer to me after pushing me away. It was a repeated move, as if I was forever on water around her, black water that constantly ebbed and flowed and which did not permit my reflection, or allow me to dock. I'd prefer to have been on firmer ground.

The envelope first:

"Dearest Thambi,

"I'm sorry about what I said to you last week. If I could take it back, I would. I want to be closer to you but I don't know how. I want to meet your mother and father but don't know how to ask. My own parents are so remote to me. It's hard to understand how you can feel so frustrated with them and drawn at the same time. Is there something wrong with me, or are you the one who's hobbled, impaired? Maybe we're both broken and that's what draws us together?

"I'd like to think it's something more than that. Look inside the box. You'll find a Nipple in a Wisconsin White skin. You remember that I suggested that colour to the line, right? I know that you don't really like the product but I hope you might get accustomed to it. I've put some music and photos and other stuff on it for you. You can even tune into ESPN on it. You just have to register on the network.
— E."

All the women at work had registered their Nipples on the Nipplework and they could conference each other electronically. I had resisted following along and nobody urged me to join; they did not really care. I opened the box and looked inside at the plastic PDA in the shape of a stylized boob. It felt curiously light. The plastic skin gleamed in an unreal shade of white as if the haze from the sun had been filtered through an atomic glaze. I could feel the words 'Made in China' embossed in the leathery skin.

So things were not completely over between Emily and myself? My desire for her had doubled while she was away on her promotional tour, and I let it flood my legs, rush forward through my fingertips. I felt my penis stiffen a little. I wanted to press my desire into the golden wax of her flesh. I wanted to bang her against the soft grey wool of the cubicle divider like in the beginning; I wanted to fight her again. But I knew it could not be so; the passion would fade if it had not already. What would be left when it burned and evaporated away – love or just a gaping black hole? I felt old and felt her to be growing old with me; I had a premonition of us as middle-aged people, dull and tired.

How could I continue seeing her while evading my father and his dirty looks? There were only so many superfluous errands I could run, so many non-existent friends that I could see, so many games I could attend. She was right – now was all we had. Unless I introduced her to my parents, nothing would move forward. The present of the Nipple, though I would never use it, was a kind gesture. I felt the kindness of her card. To be part of her life was fortunate. To be close to any woman...brought me close to tears. I had to steady myself against my desk with my elbows and put my face in my hands. How could any woman join her life to mine? Especially one so beautiful and untenable as Emily. There were no clear boundaries to anything, and I felt so delicate, so toppleable. Anybody could have pushed me over and I would have cracked.

She was right in that we had very little in common, and yet there was something there that held us, pulled us together like the magnetic lines of sex. As certain, as firm as the feel of her breast in my hand, I drew to her like a mouth to a nipple, our bodies melted and our minds drizzled and collected in the pools of sweat at each other's navels. Where was the gentle, unremote part of her where I would find my symmetry? I wished to show her my side that was caring, gentle, prone to love. It was in danger of dropping away.

I'd barely begun the day and had already lost most of my morning. Sitting here, swivelling in my chair, was no good. I grabbed my jacket and took an early lunch. So who cared if Doris and the others shouted at me? What did it matter in the scheme of things? It was only a contract job anyway. I needed good references – that was true – that was a reason to not blow things off completely.

I walked by the shawarma place where we had eaten the first time and looked through the window at the Lebanese guy with the massive pipes. I dreamed about knocking his block off. I walked on and sat on the steps outside the 401 Richmond Building. The Richmond Building. The Darling Building. The area was covered with buildings with precious names. It was as if the entire district, and not just our office, disapproved of me for Emily. Men in designer suits scurrying about with their briefcases, women with cutting-edge hair and sharp clothes, all seemed to know how I felt. *Get out of here, stranger,* they said. – She doesn't belong with someone like you. *Yes, we know you live here and she doesn't but she's one of us, and you – you're just passing through.*

Roshan was getting married. That was a fact. Emily was moving back to Montreal sooner or later. That was also a fact. I didn't know which was worse – that I didn't like Roshan's fiancée or that disliking her didn't stop me from being jealous. Why would Emily be interested in something that had no future? Why announce it to the world? To begin with, office romances are not a good idea. I didn't want to poison the well where I worked. The estrogen mafia wouldn't approve of me for her. Or her for me. Why is there so much potential for assumption, humiliation, and disappointment when people get together? Secret affairs are no better. As always, I felt like an immigrant in the land of desire. Someone is always more in desire than the other when it comes to an affair. There was something better than that, a hope that floated into view. Emily was better than that – I had to tell myself. She was not a selfish or petty person and I had to believe there was something inside her that wanted permanence, stability, and love – just like I did. I clung to this hope.

When I got back to work, I returned with a bottle of wine which I plunked down on Emily's desk. "How are you?" I said and kissed her full on the mouth. Anita and Doris and the others that weren't out to lunch gasped. I bent Emily as far back as possible by placing my hand against the small of her back. She was startled but closed her eyes and returned the kiss mid-tilt. Bless her soul – she pretended as if nothing was out of the ordinary. I let her back up and we smiled at each other. "I take it that you got my gift?" she asked.

I nodded. "The bottle's for you."

"I gathered. Is there something to celebrate?"

"I'd like to pour it all over you and lick it off drop by drop," I said.

"Thambi, control yourself," she pushed me away with one hand. "Doris, close your mouth – you look like a fish!" she said, waving Doris away with the others.

Doris closed her mouth and walked away, adjusting her glasses. Anita looked at us and shook her head. "Is there somewhere we can go talk?" I asked.

"You've already had lunch?"

I nodded. Emily closed the spreadsheet charts she had been looking at and we walked over to the washroom at the far end of the loft. We went inside and she locked the door from the inside. I kissed her again and she held me closer by the jaw before pushing me away. "Stop, what are you doing?"

"What do you think I'm doing?" I asked and grabbed her by the shoulders. She turned away and looked at us in the panel mirror. We could be seen refracted from three different angles, looking at our variegated selves.

"If I knew that it'd make you so horny, I wouldn't have made the peace offering."

"I've missed you. How was the promo trip?"

"Horrible. You don't want to hear about it. These guys don't know what they're doing. How's the wedding?"

"Horrible. They don't know what they're doing either." And then we both said, "you don't want to hear about it" in unison and looked at the floor.

"Let's talk of better things," I said, being the first to look up. I caught her eye in the mirror.

She looked away and stepped back. There was so much for the both of us to do to come closer. We were behind on everything: love, life, happiness. We strolled the errant hallways after our generation had run ahead but soon that aimless walking would come to an end. I knew it; I felt it in my bones and I refused to give in without fighting for her. I would even fight her for it. If it came to that. All the splinters and jaggedness of my bones, all the electricity in my body, would push against that boulder. I would turn the wheel of stars; I would keep hope alive.

"Forget everything that's happened between us," I said. "I don't want to be your connecting flight to some other destination. I want to be with you in a proper way. I want people to know we're together."

"I've been thinking so too." She spasmed delicately as a shudder worked up her body. "I want to meet these people who have such an effect on you."

"I'll take you to my brother's wedding if that's what it takes to make them understand," I said and pushed her against the wall. My shoulders pressed against her shoulders, my pelvis into the soft wax of her pelvis.

"Wait," she said, and stroked my neck. "Since I know about your parents, you should know about mine."

"What should I know about them?" I asked and sucked one of her fingers.

"Wait – you should know why...why I don't like to talk about them." She cleared her throat and made space for herself by wriggling free and then pushing her ass up onto the sink's ledge. I wanted to make love to her in the bathroom, amongst all the shit, all the plumbing, echoes, and toilet paper, but she wouldn't let me. She stared me square in the eye and I stood with my hands on the counter around her. I could only see the back of her now in the mirror, the outline of her bra underneath her sweater, and she launched into her tale:

"When I was seven, we lived in a walk-up in the Montreal plateau. Do you know what the houses look like there – narrow with flights of steep winding stairs? We lived on the second floor and my mother would always tell me to be careful when walking up the stairs. I held on to the metal railing and imagined my snow boots slipping and my bumping all the way to the ground – *bump! bump! bump!* my ass sore and happy as if I had sledded down a hill. My mother was a very unhappy woman in those days. She had been laid off work and moped around the house. She would pick me up from school and then it was excruciating to sit there watching cartoons while she hovered around, in her misery. I was an only child and it was just me and my mother in the house until my father came home.

"My father worked at an anglo law firm downtown and he was worried about his job too – this was the time when the PQ was pushing all the anglos out and making businesses change their signs. He was working late nights to prove he was indispensable to the firm and often came home exhausted. I ran to him and he was glad to see me but he barely had any energy left for me. I hated those long evenings with my mother, having to watch her cook some horrible macaroni and meat sauce on the stove and then eat it with her. I'm sure she drank though I didn't know it then. My father said that it was up to me to take care of my mother and that he was depending on me to make sure she was alright.

"I was only seven! And he was depending on me to make sure that my mother was alright? Is that fair? Of course, I didn't think of it like that then. I only felt a huge weight pressing down on me that I couldn't name, couldn't say whether it would go away or not. There was a day when a couple of girls, Michela Grossman and Andrea Brisbois, asked if I'd like to come over to Michela's house to play with them. I couldn't believe it! This was unusual because the other girls rarely played with me. I was an only child who clung to her father and misery surrounded us all that year. All afternoon, all I could think about was going over to Michela's to play and kept worrying about what my mom would say when she came to pick me up, and what my new friends' moms would think of my mom – I knew even then that something was wrong with her.

"Well, I needn't have worried. When my mother came to pick me up, she was drunk and late. Even I could tell that there was something different. Perhaps she was on medication too and had combined the pills with drinking? She was in her own world. She showed up forty minutes late and the other two had already left for Michela's house without me. Michela's mother left her phone number with me on a piece of paper and said that my mother could call her if it was okay to bring me over. I pleaded with her to let me go and join the other two for whatever time was left. I felt the minutes of fun rapidly draining out while I stood there pleading with my mother. My mom wouldn't listen or even let me finish. She threw the piece of paper with the phone number in the snow. I fished it out, dirty and wet, now illegible, and put it in the pocket of my parka. My mother grabbed my hand and dragged me, literally kicking and screaming, back home. She pushed me up the stairs. There was slush all over the sidewalks and stairs and I held the railing as tight as I possibly could while I climbed. My blood rushed in my head and I felt I could feel the rust dig into my palms. When we got to the landing, my mother fumbled with the keys and dropped them a couple of times. Finally, she asked me to pick them up and open the door.

"I did as she asked, but after I opened the door, I quickly slipped inside and slammed it in her face. I was so mad. Having to spend another morbid, torturous evening with her when I could be playing with my friends. I didn't even turn on the TV or eat. I just sat on the sofa as if the TV was on, my mother making some awful dinner from a box on the stove. I didn't go to the washroom – I just sat there rigid. At first, my mom banged on the door and yelled my name. I just sat there. She screamed threats and cried. "Won't you let me in? Don't you love me? I'll change – *I promise I'll change!*" I just sat there. My mother was never very persistent with anything that she did and eventually the threats and sobs subsided. The afternoon light turned to dusk that also faded and disappeared and I just remained motionless trying to drown her and the entire world out with my hands over my ears.

"My father came home. He found cops waiting for him. The cops didn't even know I was inside because there were no lights on and I hadn't responded to their knocking. Apparently, my mom had, in her drunken stupor, stumbled and fell down the stairs. I don't know how it happened but she landed head first and had been taken in an ambulance which some passerby had called for her. A witness had seen her fall and testified that it was an accident – no one was to blame. No one was to blame! If that were only the truth! Of course I was to blame and my father knew it. We never spoke about it, he never accused me, but we knew it. My mother suffered a concussion upon landing on the street and slipped into a coma. You can guess the rest."

"At least there was no suffering," I said.

"Is that right? Does a person not suffer in a coma? My father suffered. I certainly suffered. After that, things were different between us. He had to take time off work to look after me and my mother while she remained alive at the hospital but he pulled away from me. He resented me. At her funeral, he hardly spoke to me and never touched me. This is what our family has become.

"At sixteen, he happily gave me money to move away for Cegep, and I saw him a handful of times. We don't talk, we don't write. I don't keep in touch with any of my family anymore. For how long can someone hate you? How long can he keep a grudge?"

"I don't know, but it shouldn't stop you from getting close to others. You can love, you can cook, you're so talented and intelligent. You can begin things new again. Why go back to Montreal? Why not stay here?"

"This is what the marriage contract comes to, Thambi. There's something wrong with it."

I wanted to hold her in my arms but that was the mood, urging images into my head. It was obvious to me by the way she looked that she was a short push away from hating me too and anything I did would shatter the fine bubble that kept her from crying. I could see her irises shrink as if to stop the tears from coming and she was scared. Not scared of me but the future, of the interminable days that would come one after the other, repeating the torment of misery and estrangement. Knowing she was alone and that each day would be like the one before it, nothing changing, always alone.

"So you got what you wanted," she said. "Now you know."

I stepped uncertainly away from her. She was right – her worst was certainly worse than mine. My dick had gone limp and I felt cold inside. If she could do this to her mother, her kin, what could she do to me? It was true in a way that her mother had deserved it and that Emily had been a child, but what is in one's heart is true. What is true to one's person remains true to her always, does it not? She looked at me as if she could guess my thoughts. I backed away and she turned her head to follow me; I could see her refracted in three different ways. Again, in the mirror, like a stone that was broken and showed its facets. I reflected from different angles too. I thought of Rita Hayworth and her husband's many reflections at the end of *The Lady from Shanghai*. That magnificent scene where they shoot each other, all the reflections and cross-reflections of each other shattering until all their various selves are dead.

"Hey, you two! What's going on in there?" That was Gerry banging on the door. Shit! We were caught.

"I'll be out in a moment!" yelled Emily. After a while, she muttered "women's troubles!" and giggled.

"If he's in there with you..." mumbled Gerry and then walked away. I could only imagine his face colouring and the awkwardness. To work with women all day and not be able to stand up to any of them!

"Anita must have got Gerry to do this," whispered Emily. "What are we going to do?"

"What can we do?"

"I don't know – I was hoping you'd have an answer," she said.

"I'll leave first – you hide out here and leave later. Just slip out to lunch."

"I was talking about us," she said frankly, looking me in the eye.

"When I take to someone, I stick like glue."

"Glad to hear it," she cooed, her eyes sparkling.

Glad to hear it! I was going to pieces at work, even the slightest glance or murmur at work setting me on my toes, and I wasn't much better at home. Sometimes I just sat there and stared into space while cake boxes and envelopes piled up around me. "Those won't lick themselves!" said my father.

"Is something wrong?" asked my mother, taking my arm. "Something's wrong. I can tell it."

"It's just work, ma," I said. "There's a lot of stress there right now."

"Whatever it is, don't let it shake you," she said, smiling at me with worried eyes. "Be the strong person that you are!"

"I sure will," I said, and tried my best to smile.

Unstrung decorations lay all over the place. Some of the brass stands and ash and flowers that my father had picked up for the wedding lay in stacks around the apartment. It was as if we were moving out or had just moved in. We brothers had to go get our final fittings for the shervani suits tomorrow. It was hard to swallow when I thought of how much the suit would set me back. I didn't mind my mother, but the other two were really burning my ass. They had become insufferable, Roshan laughing at my father's jokes but seeming even more nervous around him. I imagined all the directions that Roshan must be pulled in. His belly would explode from the worry. Meanwhile, my mother and father seemed to chafe against each other in some unspoken way that only they could understand. This put us all even more on edge. If they only said what they truly thought, I'm sure it would have been better for all of us. The apartment had become very small and it was harder than ever to get away to see Emily. The less I could see her, the more I wanted her. The more I wanted her, the more insufferable Roshan and my father became. I tried to be gracious to them all, but God, was it hard.

After we had strung up some decorations, finally finished stamping and addressing the invitations and had sent them out and then made confirmations to pick up the wedding suits, and watched my father argue on the phone about everything along every step of the way with Lakshmi's family, it was after midnight and we went to sleep.

Roshan and I still slept in the same room and it felt too small for us and all the memories we'd had over the last seven years. Before that, we'd been in an even smaller apartment. Now, he would finally be escaping the cage into a place of his own. Lakshmi's parents had offered to put a down payment for a house in Richmond Hill for the happy couple. They would be close to Lakshmi's parents but not so close to ours. Roshan would be able to drive down whenever he could. Since the car belonged to Roshan, our parents would only be able to get there by public transit, a difficult affair once you cross into Richmond Hill.

"What were they so upset about?" I asked Roshan in the dark, both of us snuggled into our cold single beds. I had tuned out during the last hour, due to tiredness and because my mind was elsewhere.

"Appa doesn't like the idea of Lakshmi's parents giving us the down payment for the house," came his whispered reply.

"What else is new? What's his reason this time?"

"He says that it's not the proper way for us to be living so far away. He reminded us that if it was Sri Lanka, Amma and Appa would be living with us in an extended family."

"Well, this isn't Sri Lanka."

"I know," whispered Roshan, and I wasn't sure but perhaps there were a couple of almost silent wheezes; just talking about this added to his anxiety. I knew that it was all getting very hard for him. My father was finding everything increasingly difficult and complicated, and he questioned or was upset with every other thing. It seemed as if he had never had his authority questioned before. He believed in micromanaging everything. Did he not realize we were adults? What must life have been like for him back home?

"Hey," I whispered, making my voice go as quiet as possible because of Roshan's fear and my mutinous thoughts, "what do you think of Appa? Do you think he's going to sabotage everything?"

"I don't know, Thambi, I don't know," said Roshan, and he was quiet for a while. Just when I thought he might have drifted to sleep, he said, "I didn't know what to think of him coming back, but I sometimes wish we hadn't tried so hard. I'd forgotten what he could be like. You're too young to remember, but I remember him from before we left Sri Lanka. I was always terrified. Amma's a hard case but he's different. He doesn't understand. He doesn't listen. There's something mad and ferocious about him that I don't feel easy around."

This was the most we had talked in...as long as I could remember. I savoured the feeling that hung in the air. "Roshan, why did we never talk like this before?"

"There was never enough time, Thambi, there just wasn't time."

And then, lulled on by the euphoria of our moment, before I could stop myself, before I could second guess myself, I told him: "Hey Roshan, you know what scares me the most? I've started dating somebody at work and I'm scared that Appa's going to ruin the whole thing for us."

"You're dating someone! Since when?"

"I don't know. A few weeks. Maybe since around Amma's birthday."

Roshan whistled. "Props to you – what's her name? Is she pretty?"

"Emily. *I* think she's pretty."

"Look, I know I never taught you anything as an older brother. I was never there for you when I should have been, like instead of our father, but you obviously did alright."

I didn't say anything now and I felt resentful when I heard him say these things. The lull had swung back, he had become his sometimes condescending self, as if he were playing a part that was not quite sincere. "How many dates have you been on?" he asked finally.

"A few. I don't know. We spend a lot of time at her place." Despite his bluffish nature, something made me want to try and open up to him, to make myself vulnerable, to catch and hold onto this moment between us as long as I could.

"You mean you're having...?"

"Yes! Be quiet! I don't want Appa and Amma to know."

"So it's really serious. When are you going to tell them?"

"I don't know. She doesn't want to commit. Why is it that women have all the power in relationships? They decide when to move and you just have to wait until they're good and ready."

"Like Amma said before, they always did have the power – we were just too stupid to realize it."

"Do we give it away?" I asked.

"I don't know. Why – have you given all your power away?"

"I don't know."

"That's something!" He said it as if he were whistling. "You really are something! So you don't think she's going to stay with you?"

"I don't know. Women are strange. God knows whether they're going to want the same thing from one moment to the next. I mean, sometimes women will only sleep with you right away if they don't want a relationship with you. It's like that with some. If they like you, are invested, have complex feelings, then they won't want to sleep with you right away. Of course, they also won't want to sleep with you if they want nothing to do with you...I don't know anything anymore."

"Do you think she would marry you?" he asked. He really didn't understand what I was trying to explain.

"I wish I could have what you and Lakshmi have," I said after a while, "but I don't know if it's possible. She would have to leave her comfort zone to be with me. It'd be very hard on me also. God knows I'm not the most traditional Tamil but everybody would look at me differently. I couldn't take Amma being upset at me. You've already noticed that she and I don't talk as much as we used to since Appa arrived. Maybe Emily's modern enough for both of us...it wouldn't be as hard for her to break away from her roots and step into the void."

I meant the last because Emily was so distanced from her father to begin with. She had already extricated herself from the nest, whatever personal battles she had come from. But Roshan did not know anything about it. He took my meaning another way. "Of course," he said, "she's white. There is no culture to give up. She's stepping out of nothing and into nothing. And maybe in the end, who knows? – coming back to nothing."

So stupid! What had I done by opening up to him, what amnesia and insanity prompted itself upon me?

The remainder of our bond dissolved irretrievably. I pretended to drift asleep.

11

The next evening, Roshan and I stood for our second and final fittings for the shervanis – the embroidered Indian tuxedos – that were being custom made for us. The showroom of the store on Gerrard St. sparkled with lavish jackets and pants; sequined, beaded, embroidered thread shone in red, gold, pearl, and sandalwood. The waves of beauty and wealth were overpowering. What were we doing here?

I resented the fact that we were buying these shervanis and only going to use them once. At least, I was. My mother and Roshan tried to tell me that I could use mine for my own future wedding but I didn't have the heart to tell them that there would be no other Hindu wedding after Roshan's. It was almost easier to bear the cost of the gilded suit than rain on the wedding and tell them what I thought of it. Even my father did not seem to mind our spending five hundred dollars a pop on suits that would be used only once, and here he had rejected a winter jacket that cost half as much. At least he'd get use out of a jacket. He and Roshan were unspoken allies.

Later, we stood at home, dressed in regular suits and ties. I was the last one to come out of the bathroom – I must have untied and retied my tie about five times. My grizzled and overworked face looked back at me from the mirror: *what are you getting yourself into?* it asked. *This isn't like you.*

"Can you believe it?" my mother said. She stood just outside the open door to the bathroom, surveying us all. "In a few days from now, this one will be married."

Tonight was the evening of Roshan's bachelor night. My father insisted on chaperoning us, so that had put a crimp in my plans. I had to change things last minute. Instead of going down to a casino in Niagara Falls, we were going out to dinner at The Host, a popular Indian restaurant downtown. Roshan's friends were a little disappointed, but who cared? Soon, the whole thing would be over, as would the wedding, and then I could put it all behind me.

Amma and Lakshmi had never been happy about the idea of a bachelor party and were glad that our father was going to chaperone us. We didn't need chaperoning – what was the worst that we could do? It was the principle of the thing that had mattered – a last sortie for Roshan as one of the single guys. The time that Roshan and I had talked in the bedroom had left me feeling strange, angry at him for never really having been there, yet a little closer than we ever had been before, and I wanted to hold onto it as long as I could. Very soon, it would be blown to dust by his marriage. I felt guilty for neglecting that feeling too; no matter how many times Emily and I told ourselves that we were just fooling around, that it was all in good fun, every evening with her took me further and further from my family.

As if they felt it too, our parents acted strangely around each other. Amma had lost that authoritative edge of hers and my father moved slowly and sluggishly without looking us straight in the eye. He went out for the milk and came back a half hour later, not knowing which type to buy. Somewhere else, in

Thornhill, Lakshmi's plans and those of her parents proceeded exactly as they desired. It felt, deep down, as if everything we did was born out of insecurity.

"We should start thinking about Thambi's future," said my father. "Have you given it any thought, son?"

"I'm young. There are other things more important than marriage."

"Not so young," said my mother, "not so unimportant."

"I can ask Lakshmi if she knows anyone," piped up Roshan. "She asked me what type of girl you like and I didn't know what to tell her. Do you want us to look for someone for you?"

The hypocrisy of this, given what he knew about me, was startling. "You? Look for me? You can't be serious."

"Better not wait too long," advised my father. "Time has a way of flying by."

"Chi chi chi," said my mother. "Thirty years old and you can't tie a tie!" She came forward and pulled me up on my toes by the lapels of my pinstriped suit. My shoulders squeezed against my chest. She began loosening the tie and slid it around my collar as if holding me like a stone in a slingshot she wished to hurl against the world. I felt snug in her orbit and wished it was just the two of us.

"What about you and Appa?" I whispered. "I don't want to end up as unhappy as you two."

"We're not so bad," she replied, looking me in the eyes. "Survey a hundred couples and you'll come up with a hundred different problems. And they all seem like catastrophes and they all seem like they'll crack their marriages apart, but they hold on. Somehow they manage."

"Is that right though?" I asked her. "Is that a reason to stay together?"

"So what would you do? Never get married? Ha! I'd like to see you try it. We're not monks – human beings are meant to live together. Now, I know you're frustrated about the shervanis. This whole thing is costing *a lot* of money, you don't have to tell me. But it's a once in a lifetime thing and I want you to be nice to them. They'll do the same for you one day."

She sprang back and clapped her hands. "Oh, you look wonderful, all of you. Give me a kiss!"

We all gave her a kiss as we trooped out.

At The Host were Sageev, Babu, Dinesh, and Faizal, waiting for us. They cheered as we came in. They were dressed up too, although none of them were wearing suits like us. None of us had gone out to a bachelor night before and we didn't know what to do. Sageev is a dentist, Babu is a doctor, Dinesh some kind of business manager, and Faizal is an engineer. They're about Roshan's age and I call them the Four Horsemen of the Apocalypse. Babu is Indian and his name is a nickname like mine, his real name forgotten a long time ago. Faizal's parents are from Pakistan but the others are Tamil like us. It doesn't matter though, because they're all similar to Roshan in outlook – they're brown, carry on the values of their parents unquestioningly, and could stand to lose a few pounds – that's why I call them The Horsemen. Plague, war, famine, death, and the rest of it can come along in their wake and they'll be fine with it as long as their careers are secure.

The Horsemen whooped it up, brown style. They slapped Roshan on the back, played with his tie, poked him in the belly. They made him feel like an astronaut. Babu (a.k.a. plague) was married to some girl he had met in university but the others were still single. I think Dinesh and Faizal (famine and war respectively) still lived with their parents. Roshan was the first of them to take the leap and shoot into the unexplored space of arranged marriage. They had all found each other in the first year of undergrad, nerds and misfits, recognizing the hectored mien and nervous studious gaze in each other's eyes. Of course, they were drinking ginger ales and juices as we walked in. I could see it was going to be a long night.

"There he is!" Babu stood up and made way for Roshan to sit down.

"Rani let you out of the house?" asked Roshan. Our father said hello sheepishly and sat at the end. I sat even farther away, looking at them preening and enjoying each other, acting like they had never left university. They had all gone on to prestigious programs at McMaster, U of T, and York after their time together. True, I had gone to York, but I had been in the low tier of a general business program. I had taken a slew of liberal arts electives to pad my degree and Roshan had already been working by that time, helping my mother and myself, while I struggled along, pretending to be a business student.

"She's coming by later with the baby," said Babu, his puffy cheeks blowing up. When Roshan stared at him in disbelief, he yelled "psych!" and they all laughed, thrilled.

"She'd better not show up," roared Sageev, "or she'll divorce him within twenty-four hours!"

"Why – because she'll see the strippers and cocaine you guys have planned for the end of the night?" I muttered.

Our father looked at us, uncomprehending. He probably did not fully understand what I'd said but he got the gist of it.

"Thambi's upset because his plans to go to Niagara Falls fell through," said Roshan. "He's feeling a bit sour."

"Right," I answered, "I wanted this. You're always asking for things you can't get and then you're unhappy when they fall through. Why do a bachelor party at all? You're not white – you're not going to Vegas!"

"You're not white either," said Faizal, "so stop pretending that you are." Faizal was the quietest and the most intelligent of their crew.

"Let's just stop this," said Babu, the ringleader. "We're here to have fun, so let's do that."

One of the waitresses, formally statuesque and formidably beautiful in her sari, came over and took our order. She also discreetly asked us to tone it down. Other customers had complained, and a couple turned their heads towards us as she spoke.

The food arrived and we dug in. The Host does an amazing butter chicken, various paneers, lamb roganjosh, the spicy chicken vindaloo, and my favourite – malai methi machi – a roasted salmon simmered in onions and cashews. The Four Horsemen also ordered an assortment of naan, samosas, pakoras, and other things to fill up the table and their bellies. We shared and ate, all of us with expanding girths except myself and Faizal. Our father dug in hungrily – it was the first time I had seen him let go. Something of Roshan's friends must have taken him back to his own youth and his circle of friends, now scattered to the winds. I thought of Emily and the first time we had eaten together. Even if we did not set a fancy table, our yearning and attraction fed us. She shimmered and blended into the darkness so that I couldn't get a grasp on her. She was like black water, my black mermaid who was neither here nor there.

As I had told her then, North Indian food is much creamier and richer than South Indian food, as if we Tamils are serious about everything, even food itself. Now we sat in front of some of the best, richest, and creamiest in the world, but my appetite had shrunk. "Aren't you hungry?" asked my father. "I swear I'll never understand you." He shook his head.

Scooping out some of the salmon which lay on a fish-shaped serving board, I picked at it with my fork. The Horsemen were talking about what they earned. "Sageev's been promoted again," said Dinesh, "the lucky dog! At this rate, he'll be owning the place."

"Anytime you need a good accountant?" said Roshan.

"You're not happy with your place?"

"What's happy? One can always do better," said my brother.

"Speaking of which, have you heard about Sri's firm?" asked Babu. "That man is minting money."

"I always told you all that it's better to go into business for yourself," said Faizal. "You beat the whites at their own game. I don't know why I didn't listen to my own advice."

I had ordered a beer on my trip back from the washroom and was waiting for it to arrive. "You should count yourselves lucky," I said. "Some people work hard their whole lives and have nothing to show for it."

"Stop feeling sorry for yourself, we're just talking," said Babu.

"I wasn't talking about myself," I said, and folded my arms.

Our father cocked an eyebrow. He had remained quiet all this time, watching everybody, no easy feat. He was used to feeling he should be in charge and roaring his pronouncements about the world. Babu's slick mustachioed manner and sense of entitlement, easy success, intimidated our father, I think.

"If you're talking about me, don't worry" said our father. "This is why we parents came here in the first place. Not for us to succeed but for our children. Just don't forget to take care of us as we get older."

The Horsemen cast their eyes down just as the waitress arrived with my Corona. None of them could look her in the eye although they sneaked glances at her back as she walked away and gave each other secret looks and smiles. My father didn't miss any of this. "What are you drinking, Thambi?" he asked.

"A beer. Don't tell me you've never had one in Sri Lanka."

"Beer? Why would I drink beer? Your mother lets you do such things?"

"It's not up to her. You see we're all adults now – a beer once in a while won't kill you."

"It's a waste of money and a bad habit. Roshan – you also drink?"

"Why ask Roshan?" I asked. "He never does anything! Roshan – when was the last time you did anything for fun? Come on, he's not even getting married for himself, haven't you heard? Here, here – here's to Roshan and Lakshmi!" With that, I took a swig from the bottle, conscious of everybody's eyes on me. No one else partook of my toast.

"Don't mind Thambi," said Roshan, as if he was embarrassed for me. "He's used to getting his way. Our mother's spoiled him."

I took another drink from my beer to spite him. "You're just jealous because she respects me and not you."

"Watch what you say to your older brother!" warned my father.

"It's okay, Appa," said Roshan. "I can fight my own battles. You don't think I matter, huh? Who are you going to have to kick around when I'm gone?"

"Aaah – it finally comes out!" I cried. "Roshan, that's the first time I've ever heard you hint at something remotely true! You want to get out of our family as fast as you can, and I don't blame you. I'd do the same thing if I could. Unfortunately there are only two ways out for us Navaratnam boys – marriage or death! And even then, we never really escape do we? Come here – let me buy you a drink, my brother!"

I tried to extend an arm across the table but my father swatted me back. Sageev and Dinesh made as if to protect Roshan from me. I'm sure everybody was watching us. I don't know what got into me. My beer almost finished, I got up to go to the bathroom to splash water on my face. I pushed my hands through my hair and looked at myself in the bathroom mirror's reflection – I wanted to crack it with the force of my palm. Where was Emily right now? Did she think of me as often as I thought of her? God, I loved her like I had loved no one else. Was that right – was that true – was that how I truly felt? I would smash everything in my life in an instant to be with her; I would leave it all, even my loving mother, if Emily asked me to.

On the way back, I stopped at the bar and had something stronger: two vodkas neat and another beer to chase them down. It took me a while to finish them and no one came to get me. The waitress asked me how I was doing. "Lousy," I replied.

"Well, you might want to take it easy," she said. "You look like you're headed for a fall."

Advice from a waitress in a sari. Shit! God, she was beautiful. Lakshmi could only dream of looking like her. It was too bad she wasn't my type. "Give me your number?" I said, just for a joke.

She shook her head and muttered and went away.

Back at the table, the boys were talking about their jobs again. "I look at the interns," said Babu, "and just to make sure they know their place, I never compliment them on anything they do. Always cool and professional – that's me. Especially if they're white. The shoe's on the other foot now, fuckers. How do you like it? Pardon me, Mr. Navaratnam."

My father excused him with a wave of his hand but scrutinized me with a cold stare as I sat down: "And where have you been?"

"The washrooms here are excellent."

"You're a stinking...sit down and stop embarrassing us. I can't believe any son of mine," he pulled me down beside him with his rough hand.

"I told you before not to touch me," I said. "If you touch me, God help you –"

"For Heaven's sake, control yourself," said Babu. "What's wrong with you?"

"Roshan, why do you need this piece of trash in your wedding?" asked Faizal. "Brother or no brother, no one should have to put up with this." The Horsemen murmured their assent.

"If after all this time, you don't want me in your wedding – that would just be like you, Roshan. Do you know how much money I've spent on that fucking shervani?" I threw a napkin at him.

"That's it – that's enough!" And there was the stuck-up waitress with the manager beside her. The manager asked us apologetically to leave and to do it as quietly as possible. The

Horsemen – those excellent millionaires – paid for the food and shuffled embarrassedly out of there. My father picked up our coats, throwing mine at me in anger, and we trooped out.

The cold bit into our bodies as we hit the street. It didn't give us time to wrap ourselves tightly enough and the snow and frozen rain scraped against our faces as if they were icy sand. After the warmth and festivity of the restaurant, our bodies felt isolated and tight.

"Sorry it had to end early, boys," said Roshan.

"Hah! What were all you bad boys going to do anyway – go to a strip club?" I yelled.

They ignored me and said their goodbyes to Roshan, hugging him before they departed. They left him emptier, smaller than he had been at the beginning of the night, and he stared after them with misery and uncertainty, not knowing what to do. I could imagine him wanting to run after them. This should have been a last hurrah, a remembrance and full farewell to those undergrad days he had never truly grown out of, and I had wrenched the night from beneath his feet before he could experience it.

My father did not hesitate to tell me this. "I can't believe you," he said. "How did any son of mine become so pathetic? You're a drunk and you smell like one. Don't you have any manners? You could learn something from those boys."

"When I need your advice, I'll ask for it," I said.

We carried our sourfacedness and resentment all the way down the street, the wind howling past our frostbitten ears. Our hair was damp with sleet. Water and broken ice lay all over the sidewalk. Other people caroused and walked by us, happy. Underneath our feet, patches of ice loomed dark and slick like pieces of the night sky that had broken and fallen from the heavens. I wished that I could pick one up and throw it. Or jump into one and disappear.

Roshan ran to catch up with me and grabbed me by the shoulder. He almost slipped. "What the hell is wrong with you?" he asked. "What was that all about?"

"All what?" I pushed his hand away.

"You know what I'm talking about. Why did you act that way? It was embarrassing."

I turned around and stared at him cold. Our father too had stopped now in his tracks. We formed a triangle in the snow. We could have been Clint, Lee, and Eli in *The Good, The Bad, and the Ugly* with Roshan being the Ugly. "Do you think it's a pleasure to be talked about that way by you and your buddies? Do you think it's a pleasure for me to set all this up for you and then have you condescend to me?" I retorted.

"Nobody's condescending you. Sure – those guys are going to talk about their careers – what, are they going to talk about art and poetry? There's no need for you to feel inferior. If you gave more of yourself, you would get more out of life."

"You piece of shit, this is exactly what I'm talking about." I bit my fist to keep myself from hitting him. "This is exactly what you said to me a few weeks ago about my job. I may not be a big piece of shit manager like you but I'm happy with myself."

"See – this is the way he talks to me," said Roshan to our father. "Can you believe the way he speaks to me? What do you think?"

"Thambi, I'm really seeing another side of you tonight. Drinking, talking like this. Aren't you ashamed?" asked our father for what must have been the third time that night. "Up until now, I thought you had some bad habits but now you show yourself to be twisted," he said, shaking his head.

"I told you to stay out of it," I replied. "If Roshan has a problem, he can take it up with me. He doesn't need to hide behind your shirtsleeves."

Our father tried to take my hand, saying, "Come on. Too much drinking..."

I shook him off and squared my shoulders, ready to fight: "I told you not to touch me."

"Just leave him alone, Appa. Same old Thambi. He acts big but it doesn't mean anything."

I made a jab at Roshan with my fist and he ducked it easily.

"Is that a joke? Was that supposed to scare me?" asked Roshan. "Let me tell you about this one, Appa. Just so you understand who he really is." Roshan walked behind me as if to prove that he had nothing to worry about. He grabbed me by the shoulders and shook me. I stood my ground and faced forward at my father, trying my best to prove that I was not rattled. "This one has always gotten away with whatever he wanted when it comes to our mother. I'm marrying a girl from a good family with a good reputation because it'll be good for our family...but not this one. Do you know why he really wants to get out of the house in the evenings? Do you know where he goes? It's not to sports games. He has a white girlfriend that he sleeps with. The whole thing...He doesn't care!"

I wheeled around and slapped him. I felt the heel of my palm strike his cheek, hard enough to crack bone. Unfortunately it didn't. It glanced off his nose and a trickle of blood slid out, black in the moonlight, and dripped steadily to the snow. My hand felt sticky and warm. It stung with shame and I smeared the blood between my fingers.

"Don't you dare touch him...", the last words like a sob in the icy wind, barely audible. I wheeled around. Was this our father, his face distorted with fear? The features cut in half by fresh pain; it seemed as if his nose and mouth had slipped. In his wordless howl, one end of his mouth rose higher than the other. I couldn't understand why he reacted this way because it was Roshan I had struck.

"How dare you?" he asked me. "How can you dare to treat your older brother that way? If I had treated my brother this way...if I had talked to my parents the way you talk to me...what will we do now? Tell me, is this true – is this true?

You're sleeping with her? How will you get married after this? How will you recover your reputation? How can you..."

There were no words to describe his despair. I didn't know what to say and Roshan nursed his bloody nose, in hiding and waiting to see what happened. "And what if I don't want to get married?" I weakly asked. "What if I never want to get married?" I had begun to take Emily's line.

"I never thought in a thousand years," said my father at last between sniffles when he had found his voice, "my own son could do this...what are you to me now? What will people say? I never imagined...what has your mother let you do – what have things come to? You've broken my heart. How can you participate in your brother's marriage like this?"

"My girl has nothing to do with the rest of you," I said. "Leave her out of this. I love her. I don't know if I'll marry her but I know what love is. It's a feeling you could never understand. And just because you don't understand, it doesn't mean I'm going to let you have your way."

"Your mother and I *do* love each other. We may not say it but we do. It's not so easy for me to talk like you – so freshly, so blatantly – it's not as easy for me to change masks for each person that I meet. I'm a father and this is all I have left. If I don't have you – my wife and children – what do I have? Do you know how much I've been through in my life? I've lived through horrors you couldn't imagine. You can feel the fracture line in my head if you like. Here!" He pointed at his right temple. "I may not be perfect, I may not have been there, but whatever I did, I did for you. If not you, whom? The only thing that's kept me going is the thought that we might all be reunited one day. And now this. How am I to believe it?" He raised both hands to his temples as if I had now cracked him on the left side of the skull to match the blow from the scurrilous agents years ago.

I felt as if I had knocked him back over the ocean. "Well, believe it," I said staunchly. "She is mine and I am an adult, no matter how many parents say otherwise. I will go to her and drink her love and if you don't approve, you can go fuck yourself."

"What are you saying?"

"I will move out and so help me God, I will run away with her."

"You can't be serious!" He made a grab for my arm. "Come on. Let's forget this nonsense. We'll pretend it never happened. Let's get back home."

"I told you not to touch me, and don't talk about her that way. I'm going to see her now, whenever I want." I shoved him away with my arm and he fell backwards on a black patch of ice. He splayed his arms out to stop himself and then collapsed onto the ice. A fresh tremor of pain shot through his face. Even his hair twitched. Roshan walked around me to help him but our father had difficulty standing up.

"Thambi, help me!" cried Roshan, but I was sick of listening to Roshan by now. For the first time, I wondered whether I was truly drunk. My knees went wobbly and the ice seemed to shimmer. Was I that bad at holding my liquor? I had made a promise to them both about my love for Emily and it was only tonight, after I voiced my feelings in such precise, hallowed terms that I seemed to feel them for the first time. I realized who she was to me, that I felt more strongly about her than I ever had about anybody else, and didn't understand why it was then so difficult for us to connect. My knees shook and my throat heaved and all I knew was that I had to get out of there.

"I'm going," I said.

I turned around and ran, taking care to avoid the puddles. I will remember this moment for the rest of my life because, despite Roshan's shouts, despite the howling wind, I swear I heard my father cry out for me one last time before his soul cracked. One last gust of a plea wrenched from his throat, a low warble of sobs pleading me to stay and fall back to the life that we had known. "Thambi!" His cry hovered out in the thin air, clear as a bell sounding my name. I did not turn back. I ran to the subway and to Emily's cold, stark apartment.

12

I stumbled up the subway steps and over to Emily's street. The rain had thoroughly invaded my muffler and jacket now and chilled my heart to the core. My heart had become as hard as the ice I saw my father sliding down onto, again and again. It was as black as the sky and the poison brewing within it in the place of clouds, as black as the venom that ran through our family's history. Here it was, the alleyway that led below Emily's apartment.

Crooked plywood boards were still strewn beside the bags of garbage. The wood creaked beneath my weight as I stepped into the alley. Was that the smell of soiled clothes and rotting cabbage? I imagined her sweet sweet skin's smell of olives and warm milk, something to come home to. The homeless had slept here, right below my lady's window. The rain hammered against the brick soot and bounced onto the cast iron railings of the fire escape. What if she was not home? I had not called but I could hear music from her second floor window, the lights dimmed. I thought I saw the glow of her laptop screen pulsating there. I could smell the garbage as the steam from sewer vents warmed it and blew it through the mouth of the alleyway. What if she was home but refused to see me? What if she left me out on the doorstep until I took the only choice I had? Return home in humiliation. I didn't know whether it was a strong decision or a weak decision to come see her like this.

Braving the frozen boards that lined the alley, I made it over to the fire escape ladder that descended from her 'balcony'. She had no balcony – only the landing of the fire escape in all its rusted glory. During the summer she might have put flowering plants out there, chrysanthemums and begonias, but there was nothing up there now except the frozen bars that lay like a stage for rutting cats. The better yet to howl my song into the night and announce my presence to her. I rubbed my gloveless fingers vigorously and blew on them. Then I hauled myself up the rungs.

I banged on the window. The music was turned down and steps shuffled into the room. The light turned on. "Who's there?" she asked.

It was still pretty dark out where I was. And cold. "It's me," I replied and knocked rhythmically on the glass.

Slowly, the window opened, the old soaked wood creaking against the stiffness of the ice.

"What are you doing here?" she asked with arms crossed against the cold, or against me, I could not tell.

I imagined her like Juliet in the balcony scene of some high school play long forgotten. Unlike the eponymous heroine, she allowed me in, less enthusiastically, and me a waterlogged Romeo. Though she came with no importuned speech, and all she had to give me was a towel as I sat on her sill and dried myself off, she was no less beautiful than the sun. I was ready to throw off my clothes and leap into the warmth of her bosom, the heart which burned there so crisp, to fry myself to a lump of coal, a cinder. The day had been full of ups and downs and it was not over yet.

"It's broken," I said.

"What's broken?"

"Everything. All I have left is you. That's why I came here."

"I don't understand," she said, and then made me tell her everything. I told her about the arguments – all of them, as best as I could remember – my father's fall, my running away to meet her. My words to him like a spit in the face. I wanted to run away with her now.

"I've got news to tell you too, Thambi," she said. "Though this won't come as much of a surprise to you, I'm sure. I was going to tell you at work, but given the way they stare at us, this is better."

"Go on."

"The Nipplework has finally been shot in the head. It happened today. After all the problems, the server crashed five times today. All the booster support over the last few weeks, the extra cash and PR being poured in...nothing! All for nothing. They're declaring bankruptcy."

"That's it? What's happening to Doris and the people at work, all those who've bought them and registered?"

"The phone line's going to be supported by another carrier while they declare chapter seven bankruptcy. During that time, some people will get their money back."

"And the others?"

"I don't know. I don't know what happens to them. I feel awful about it."

"I didn't know," I said, shaking my head. "I didn't know it was that bad."

"We all knew...but we didn't want to admit it. Once you get beneath the surface novelty of the product, there's not much there. It's made my job hell in the last few weeks. Very difficult to promote."

Her frankness was disarming. She could just as easily have been talking about our relationship. There was an air about her...exacting, final, distant, that allowed me inside her apartment but not the innermost recesses of her heart. She was different from the last time we talked. Certain expectations had been laid out. But nowhere in them was it said that I could crawl into her apartment unannounced. Was she speaking in double entendres? We had done things in secret for so long that lingering smiles, caught glances, and flashing winks had become our language. With things forced into the open, we did not know how to talk.

Well, I would do one better than crawl into her apartment. I would crawl into her life. For there was nowhere else for me to go. I had cut the ties that bound me for most of my life; I was cast loose in the raging storm that blew outside, swirling the garbage and sheets of ice down below, and for the first time, I did not want it any other way.

"So what does this mean for you?" I asked, facing her directly, my head thrust forward. She wore an old sweater with a bra strap poking out over her angular shoulder. Her hair fell in disappointment, no longer buoyed by the sparks and flashes of her career's most promising project. If even a little of me was the smallest bit glad, I did not admit it.

"This means I have to go back to Montreal. I'm going to say goodbye to all of you at work on Monday."

"There's no other way?"

"Not if I want to keep my job."

"And what about us? You said the last time we talked," I had to steady myself against her freezing sill, "you said that you were sure now – we would be together."

"Oh, Thambi," she came over and tried to hug me. I did not resist her but I did not reward her either. It was the first time she had softened this evening, but something deep in me wanted more. She finally let go and straightened, looking me in the eye. "I meant it with all my heart, but what can we do? I have no contract here anymore and after you kissed me in front of everyone at the office I doubt I have any friends there either. What am I to do? I love you but I've never given up my professional life for someone else. I never will."

"Don't. Don't say those words together."

"What words?" she asked innocently.

"Don't tell me you love me and in the same breath refuse to do anything about it. Love isn't love if it cannot act. It's love that says it's love only..."

"Then what do you suggest? Be practical, my dear; suggestions are called for, not sentiment."

"If you can't give up your job, I can give up mine. It doesn't matter to me. I was only hanging on to make ends meet. I was miserable until I met you. Wait for me – I can go back to Montreal with you."

"And do what?" she asked, placing her hands on her hips. "Thambi, Thambi – do you know what things are like there? There are no jobs unless you speak French. How good is your French? And who will you spend time with? My anglo father who wants nothing to do with me? How do you think he will take to you? They have had it in for people who are not French, never mind non-white, since the sixties. You wouldn't even be an anglophone – they've got a whole other category for you. You think you're discriminated against here? Wait till you get to Quebec!"

"One of the coasts, then!" I threw my arms up in exasperation. "We can both get basic jobs on the East or West Coast. I'd love to hear the pound of the ocean. I'd toil in a store or a factory to come home to you at the end of the day. Why not – other generations have done it. Or we can run away to another country, a country where we'll fit in for who we are, where people won't look down upon us. We're young. We don't need anybody else."

She took her hands off her hips and turned the palms up. "Where is that country, Thambi? What is its name?"

She was right. She was so right, and she knew that I knew it. Coming forward, she took my head in her arms and kissed the top of my head. It felt wet and icy where her lips touched me, despite the general condition of being wet to my very soul. I was made of ice and water. If she held me any closer, I would crumble, my shape would collapse and run all over her dark apartment floor.

She kissed my ear and then said, "I want to repair my job, not run away from it."

"Don't you love me anymore?" I whispered, not daring to look at her.

"I don't know. I still feel the same things I did yesterday but now everything is so different. Your parents know. Everybody at work knows. Somehow our love seems diminished."

"I still have enough love for the both of us," I said.

"That's not how it works," she whispered back, and kissed me longingly on the cheek.

Now I felt confused. The kiss warmed my face; I could feel her mouth on the other side of my tongue, through the skinny tight flap of my cheek. At the same time, I felt all the air in my birdchested frame go out. What was she saying? Was it over? Was this it? If you say this is it, I'm gone, I thought. *I have nowhere to go. I left my father crying in the street for you. Is this all there is? Is this all?*

She sensed my feelings, for she relaxed and let go, held me in front of her as if inspecting a cut on my face, the wound made visible. She turned me this way and that to assure herself that I was really there, barely more than a hundred and forty pounds of me, soaking wet. Satisfied, she let go and dusted her hands. "Look, we should get some sleep," she said. "We'll sort it out in the morning. Make yourself comfortable on the couch. I'll prepare some bedding for you. I've still got some notices to sort out over here. Damage control after all that's happened today." She pointed at the laptop.

Blankets and a bed sheet were fetched for me from her linen cupboard. She pulled one of the pillows from her bed. I did not help her as she unfolded and stretched these things out on the sofa. She had a black leather sofa in her living room, a dark well under the quicksand of her walls. More a showpiece than a bed. I had never had to sleep there before. But then I had never slept over before either. She could always kick me out, I supposed. One must be grateful for small mercies. I looked at her longingly while she set it all up. She did not look back but must have felt my eyes bore into her sweater and the second skin of her black leggings. I knew she was not happy because she did not say goodnight when she left me and closed the bedroom door behind her. Then I heard nothing, not even music, come out of that room. She had disappeared into her black box.

There was nothing left for me but to strip to my boxers – the rest of my clothes were wet anyway – and slide between the sheets. The lights were off and I was surrounded by as much darkness as unfamiliarity. My mind was clouded, my entire life was in darkness – I did not know what would happen in the morning. Would we be friends or enemies? I sat up in the dark, my mind racing, my chest pounding, but that soon became uncomfortable too and I put my head back onto the clammy leather of her armrest.

There was the whirr-whirr of a ringing sound. The sound of my own phone startled me at first but it was a welcome diversion. I fished it out of my suit's pocket and looked at the screen. *Roshan!* My erstwhile brother was texting me. It would be good for a laugh. I read the incoming text, the only light a burst of orange playing across my puckered face.

"Thambi, wher the hell r u, you fucking idiot? Do u know what's happnd 2 Appa? Fractured finger. All because of u! Good work!"

I read it over again. And then again. Again. Again. I must have read those hundred characters over and over until the battery on my phone finally died out. All along, it never occurred to me to move from the couch or to text him back. What could I say? What would I ask? "Sorry...please forgive me?" I felt the final blow, the last whisper of his hissing voice across the night, my chest shatter into a thousand pieces. If Roshan had wanted to win, he had finally found a way to do it. What could I say at this point? It did not matter whether I had fled or he had kicked me out. My world was in pieces anyway, and somehow, that night, within a span of hours, a mighty foot had kicked me free from every safety I knew. It had shaken the firmament and kicked me across space.

Weeping seemed futile. Contrition seemed futile. I was perfectly cast off and I had helped myself to it.

Of course I could not sleep now. I tried to stroke myself to ease my pain. I imagined that if I could come just once, all the tension would slip out of my body and I would be able to sink into sleep. The tension was there and I was as stiff as a candle. I imagined her there in the next room, only metres away from me. I could have broken down her door, and swept her up in her sweater and leggings. I didn't even need to imagine her with her clothes off – that was the power she had over me. I began to stroke as slowly and quietly as possible, so as not to let on, so that she wouldn't hear, but I couldn't do it. A thousand thoughts swarmed through my head. What if she heard me? What if I spilled seed across her blankets and she noticed the next morning? The shame! *The shame!* I tried to continue while lifting the sheets away with one hand but I was uncomfortable. I was as stiff as a pole but nothing would come; I was too rigid and the pain was gathered there. It hurt. I tried to imagine Emily taking off her clothes but all I could think about was my father lying there in the street, his hand shattered. Because of me. I tried to think of Emily but instead I thought of my father.

Unbidden, a memory came back to me. When I was very young, I was at the beach with my father. Barefoot, the sand in Sri Lanka, a sparkling white. The roll of the waves and the spume, the warm tropical air and the breeze. Coconut trees leaning toward the water, over the sand. My father carries some meat from the market, wrapped up in wax paper and string. The package is smooth and glazed, it reflects the sun.

Somewhere, out of nowhere, I have cut my foot. Somehow, some sharp object, a piece of glass, a rock, something, has found itself in my skin. It is not just a cut but a gash. I feel like I can smell my own blood, I can taste it on the air, and it makes me dizzy. The soft flesh, the padding underneath my sole has been cut. I start to go down. My father is there in an instant. Appa lifts me up, holds me with his hip, balances me against his shoulder. He bucks me up and smiles. Eases the pain. Talks to me. What is he saying? At first, he drops the meat but then he picks it up with his other hand. He finds a flat place and sits us down there, nudging away the hurt. And then the astonishing thing, he sucks on the wound. He holds the wound in the foot closed and with his other hand, unties the package. The cold meat comes out and is applied to my foot. Then throwing away the meat, he takes the wax paper and wraps it around my foot and uses the string to tie it up. He has big fingers, is clumsy, nervous not to show his fear. Does not do a very good job wrapping my foot. The wax paper crackles against my leg, sliding uncomfortably, the string is messy and caught up. The blood falls away to the sand. I love him for it anyway.

Funny I should have forgotten this till now. How old was I – three? To this day there is no scar on my foot, it does not work any less well for whatever happened. A child's flesh will grow back. If only I was a child, if only my heart would grow back so easily. Why do I think of this now? Why can I not love myself? That rotting meat left on the beach with my blood, the piece of glass that cut me. The rustle of wax paper.

I could not come but I uncertainly drifted off to sleep. That couch was a coffin of black in the sea of sand. I dreamt myself running across hot Egyptian deserts with nothing but a black sky above me, not even a guiding star. The sand sucked at my legs, threatening to swallow me in. My heart pounding like an organ in a canopic jar, struggling to get out.

"Thambi, wake up." Emily shook me. "You were screaming."
"What time is it?"
"It's early yet. Come to bed with me." She took me by the hand and pulled me up, out of the quicksand and onto the floor. The night was as thick as ink. I pushed myself up from the couch with my free hand, allowed her to lead me to the

bedroom. From here on in, whatever she said went. I had no idea about anything. She could glue me back together or she could break me apart.

It was all the same.

I did not think to tell her about the text that I had received. She pulled me onto the bed that I knew so well, that was now as familiar as my own, and pulled my boxers down and off my legs. I mechanically lifted her sweater over her shoulders and then pulled away the bra over her arms without lovingly taking care to undo the clasps as I preferred. Tease the moment out. She kicked off her leggings herself. The damn computer was still on and its phosphorescent glow bathed us so that we were making love under alien light. The Eye of Horus blinked at me knowingly from her ankle, like an ancient computer cursor waiting for me to fail. I imagined myself in the beak of Horus flying over the Egyptian desert.

"I want you inside me," she said. "I'm wet. I want you to come inside me."

I was erect again. When had that happened? For a second, I imagined her getting pregnant. She'd have to stay with me then. We'd have a family. A happy nuclear family. We'd have to make a go of it. If circumstances worked that way. If there's anything I've learned about circumstances, it's that they rarely work the way you want.

She held me gently and guided me towards her. All the pain and the knottedness of an hour ago flooding back – I could feel it tight, right there at the base. The pain was unbearable. I was stiff but I was not going anywhere. She tried once and then moved herself, propped a pillow beneath her. She tried again and then moved me by pulling my shoulders, a little too forcefully. No good. I could not enter her. For the first time since that first night, our angles were all wrong. We were incompatible. That was it. Game over. The throbbing inside me urgent like a jackhammer to my groin, to my head. It had built up in slow waves from a murmur to a sharp electronic drill. I no longer wanted to make love but the pain was unendurable. The light from the computer flattened her out, her skinny body, her washed out hair, even her face had changed shape. The beautiful vase had become a gourd.

"It doesn't matter," she said sympathetically. "...I don't know if I have any carrots left in the fridge."

It wasn't making love at all. It was making do. It was the feel of waxed paper.

I got up. I put on my boxers and found my suit. I put my pants on one leg at a time. My damp shirt. The shoes. I went into her bathroom and tied the tie, a dispirited echo of earlier that evening when my mother had been watching and talking to me. I put on the jacket and the coat. She had put on some clothes of her own. She watched carefully from against the wall, not trying to stop me, assuming that I was ready to leave by the door.

I surprised her. I left the way I had come in. I opened her bedroom window and climbed out onto the icy fire escape. My palms ragged and scratched from earlier. The wind howling. It rained needles and glass. A cat screeched somewhere. I balanced on the edge of the railing, her 'balcony' above the garbage. The cold ice bit into my ass, my palms. I thought of the flowers there during the springtime, myself as Romeo in that scene from the high school play. I perched on the edge of that railing, the balance so precarious like a tightrope above my life, plywood boards and garbage below. It took my total concentration to balance there, against the sleety rain and wind. I couldn't think of anything else; I had to hold my total concentration on that one spot to stay perched.

Emily came out through the window, onto her 'balcony'. She drew her sweater around her. I could hear the soft footfalls of her slippers behind me, smell her smell of vinegar and olives, that oily perfume of her skin.

"What's wrong?" she asked, tapping me on the shoulder.

What wasn't?

I let go and I jumped.

13

I woke up in the ambulance, in pain. Emily called 911 but she would not ride to the hospital with me. Understandably perhaps. The paramedic patted my head back down onto the stretcher and eased me back into unconsciousness.

The parabolic arc as I plummeted into all that trash. For a second, a sense of being lifted off the ground, not falling. Yet fall I did, from Emily's life right back into my own. The space between lives, between moments, the first time in months that I'd felt free from having to control everything – an ounce of pleasure shot through my veins.

Again, I woke up at the hospital, was rushed through a round of x-rays, and had this plaster cast applied like a cocoon to my leg. I've got it for five more weeks. What kills me more than the cast, more than the two crutches over there against the wall, more than the swinging gait I've become accustomed to, is the sight of my naked toes sticking out the bottom of my cast. So vulnerable and I can't do anything about them. It seems as if my heart rests upon those toes; no matter what I do, I can't kick it back up, into my chest. Despite my best efforts, the x-rays show that it is not a debilitating injury. The fibula, near my right ankle, is cracked in three places. There is a hole there the size of a nose stud. Three lines the width of a hair extend from that ragged hole across the lower ball of the fibula where it joins the foot. If you squint at it just right, it appears to be a shadowy Eye of Horus, the disintegrating shade of Emily's tattoo. I always thought of myself as imprinting my desires into the soft wax of her flesh but instead, it was her shape which chipped its way into my bones. What part of me left through that fractured hole, escaped through the eye of that needle? I count my stars that I did not have to undergo surgery, that I escaped the scalpel knife.

My mother, deeply worried, was the only one who came to pick me up at the hospital. The horror and alarm on her face was apparent as they wheeled me out in a wheelchair. I pushed myself up out of the chair as forcefully as I could and hoisted myself up, a stork upon crutches. Amma didn't know whether to take my arm or not, how much she should help, and this was how we stumbled out. She had never gotten her driver's licence and we had to take the subway back to Scarborough and then a cab. Roshan wouldn't even drive to the carport at Kennedy station – that's how angry he was.

They were all alarmed when they saw me – Appa, Roshan, even Lakshmi. What could we do – the wedding was only a few days away – we had to keep going. To keep from falling apart, I downplayed things, insisted on doing everything myself, including washing and dressing. My mother and I kept glancing away from each other to keep from weeping. I said that I had slipped on the icy stairs and fallen. We never discussed what had really happened. The flimsy story mirrored what had happened to my father; it eclipsed what had been going on with Emily.

Why did I let go? If I could answer that one, I wouldn't be here, would I? We're near the end of our sessions and I'm no closer to an answer. Perhaps this – looking like this – was the only pragmatic way for me to face my family after what I'd done. The yakuza principle of severing the pinky in atonement. Perhaps it was a way to garner sympathy, as Roshan says, a last ditch attempt to scrounge up what remained of the emotional spotlight in the face of his wedding. Perhaps. The hospital wants you to write a report to make sure that I am no danger, either to myself or others. Danger? When is a person not dangerous to himself or others? Especially where men and women are concerned. To be alive and rub shoulders with someone else is dangerous – don't you agree?

Back to the wedding. It was only a few days away. There were a thousand and one things to be done. The boxes with the cakes were still not assembled. All of the coconuts and the bananas and the incense and the camphor and the utensils for the ceremony had been bought but had not yet been taken to the hall. At one point, my father asked Roshan to drive to the Tamil store to pick up twenty betel leaves and Roshan mistakenly came back with twenty beetroots. Relatives and friends of relatives who had driven in had to be accommodated. Visitors and well-wishers paraded through the apartment and calls kept the phone ringing off the hook.

The wedding. Finally, the day of the wedding (or the 'weeding' as the priest pronounced it). Lakshmi was being prepared: washed, made-up, saried at her place with her mother, her parents' relatives, and various other women in her party. Roshan's tholan (a cousin of Lakshmi, as she had no brother) arrived at our place along with an uncle of theirs to help wash and dress Roshan and welcome him into the family. We dressed in the shervanis that had been bought for the occasion. I had to cut off the right leg of my white pants which came with my shervani so that I could fit my cast through. The ragged edge had to be folded down and held in place with a rubber band as there was no time for new tailoring. My father sneered but the trivialities were momentarily forgotten as cars arrived to escort us to the wedding. He beamed with pride in his cream silk kurta that was less ostentatious than Roshan's shervani, but nevertheless made him dignified and serene, as he and Roshan sailed out the door.

Mr. Ramlanathan drove my mother and myself to the banquet hall where the ceremonies were to be performed. Roshan and our father went ahead with the tholan. Ramlanathan, grateful for having been invited, but more than that, joyous at weddings, had brought his niece, a mousy serious thing. We had attended her wedding the previous summer. Half a year and already the post-matrimonial bliss had sailed out of her. She looked from side to side as if searching for her husband, unsure whether he might show up and surprise her. It took a while for me to get fixed up in the back seat after having navigated the treacherous ice that lay on the sidewalk.

My crutches went in the trunk and my mother sat beside me. Ramlanathan chattered on about all the weddings he'd been to over the last few years and my mother replied in solemn nods and assents, facilitating him to go on with his happy recollections. The conversation was mostly held by them; the Ramlanathan niece, Sarojini, seemed preoccupied and I stared out the window as if I was seeing the wintry landscape for the last time, as if we were not going to a wedding but leaving the country instead.

For some reason, I expected people to look my way as we entered the capacious banquet hall. I expected them to see me hobbling in on crutches like a benighted brave soul, cheer for me, clap raucously. This did not happen. A few guests were milling about; most were already seated and had started to munch on the vaddais and the pakoras and the other snacks that were being served to them. There were thirty-five tables with numbers and a glass vase with roses in the centre upon each of them. Down the middle ran a walkway with wicker arches that had flowers entwined upon them. The wedding parties would walk down the carpet that stretched from the lobby, under these arches, and to the raised dais at the front of the hall. Beside the dais stood a three-foot wedding cake to the right and the hired DJ to the left. The DJ played a lighthearted mix of classic Tamil songs and modern Indian pop. On the dais, where the long, slow wedding ceremony would take place, sat a couple of high-backed ornate wooden chairs with embroidered seats and detailing, surrounded by pillars and a canopy with a lotus motif. Roshan and Lakshmi's cousin were seated on the chairs, performing the initial part of the ceremony. They seemed tired and nervously scanned the hall, their eyes darting from one guest to the other, muttering the odd word without turning to face each other. Despite his dents and knocks, Roshan was quite regal in his gold and red embroidered shervani. He looked like a maharajah of old. Before the chairs sat the priest in a glowing white cloth, overseeing the rites with the panoply of coconuts, bananas, flowers, vessels, camphor, incense, and other offerings that were his stock in trade. Beside his folded legs lay his ubiquitous black cellphone.

Due to my injury and the inconvenience I had caused, I was no longer part of the wedding party. Placed at the back with the Ramlanathans, the five hundred dollar suit had gone to waste. I sat down beside Mr. Ramlanathan who seemed pleased to have my company. My mother immediately began to visit the tables, one by one, to say hello to the guests. Luckily, my accident had released me from having to hobnob and I could sit there, kept company by the ecstatic Mr. Ramlanathan. "Ramesh wanted to come," he said (Ramesh being Sarojini's husband), "but his company works extra hours in the Christmas season." Apparently, Ramesh worked for some kind of retail distributor. "And my wife wanted to come too but she has another wedding to go to, can you believe it? But I didn't want to miss your brother getting married. So I said to her: you go to that one and I'll go to this one. *Hee hee.* You know, I can remember both of you when you were very little. You used to like to read. Can you remember that? Sometimes, I would visit your house and your mother would have Roshan serve us soft drinks. And then I'd ask 'where's Thambi' and she'd say 'he's reading. All the time, I don't know what he's reading! I don't know what to do with that boy!' Are you still reading sports magazines and such?"

"Not so much," I said. What he described sounded right. I used to read and shut my door so as to avoid guests and their inane questions. What I didn't know was that you never grow too old to outgrow guests and their questions. People came over to ask me about my leg and how it was healing. They were in good spirits and as soon as they heard that the injury was not permanent, they quickly went on to what they'd really been meaning to ask: *So when are you getting married? – When will it be your turn? – You have to act quickly, you know – You're not getting any younger – We want to come to your wedding next time!*

I looked away as they asked me these questions, focused on the vase of roses at the center of the table. The cut glass vase was elegant; it reminded me of Emily's vase-shaped head. For an instant, the rose petals looked like her hair, the pattern on the glass looked like her eyes. Her face with the elegant nose and all of its beauty shimmered into view. I wanted to lift up the vase with my hands and smash it to the ground. But I calmed myself, forbore the inane questions of my interlocutors. What would I say? *I am too passionate to marry! Bring me the head of Emily Vale! Let me plant flowers in her eyes!* What would be the good in that?

Finally, it was time for the bride's party to arrive. Lakshmi, holding a large garland of carnations, marigolds, and other flower blossoms, came out in a pink and green brocade sari that I have to say was quite rich and stunning. She looked incredible in it and her hair was coiffed up like a waterfall that poked at the gold veil that hung over her head. A retinue of women and relatives accompanied her slow march down the carpet and into the hall. Two small girls skipped ahead of them, holding flowers, while her father, the only male, soberly stood at her side. They walked in a stately procession down the carpet and underneath the arches until Lakshmi ascended the dais and placed the garland of flowers over Roshan.

He took the veil off her head and he, in turn, took a gold wedding necklace that was handed to him and placed it over Lakshmi. The others on the dais, including my parents, picked up flower petals and rice and showered the happy couple. My father, with his damaged mitt, cracked a smile and gleefully aimed a handful of rice at his son and daughter-in-law. "You should go up," said Mr. Ramlanathan.

I shook my head. "Later," I said.

This was only the beginning of this stage of the ceremony. Directed by the priest, Roshan now placed a garland around

Lakshmi's neck. And then another set of garlands was placed. Their helpers, the tholan and the tholi, helped them with the proceedings and straightened the flaps of their sari and turban and stood by their sides. The couple then each took one garland off from around their necks and exchanged them. With all the switching, I became dizzy watching them.

The priest gave a tumbler of milk to Lakshmi. She spooned milk out onto a leaf which Roshan held in his hands. Roshan drank the milk. She dolloped out a few more spoonfuls and Roshan drank again like a good little boy. I knew that Lakshmi did not want to talk to me after what had happened after Roshan's bachelor night. Our father was as responsible for ruining it as I was, but he would never understand that or see things that way, and neither would Roshan, so I was the one left feeling guilty.

Roshan and Lakshmi then got up out of their seats and Roshan placed a ring on Lakshmi's big toe on her right foot. The four of them linked hands: the tholan, Roshan, Lakshmi, and the tholi, and then they all walked around the edge of the dais. Roshan placed a ring on Lakshmi's left big toe. They walked around some more, Roshan's right hand gaily swinging Lakshmi's right hand so that they walked almost diagonally to each other. The priest finally got up and placed a bucket of water and flower petals in front of the couple. The tholan handed the priest a ring and the priest threw the ring into the bucket. The object was for the bride and groom to stick their hands into the bucket and see who could fish out the ring. They rolled up their sleeves and pushed their hands in. To my surprise, Roshan found it almost immediately and triumphantly pulled it out.

Just then, the priest's cellphone began ringing. He looked at it on the dais beside the coconuts and then, as if it was the most natural thing in the world, answered it. I could only imagine what he was saying: 'Listen to me...think about what we talked about...why do you worry?' The rest of them waited there, Roshan and Lakshmi crouched by the bucket, while he answered his call. The priest nodded his head as if it were God himself who had phoned down to tell the priest that he was doing a superb job, officiating on His behalf. Roshan and Lakshmi looked at each other, dark moods beginning to overshadow their faces. I imagined someone on the other end telling the priest, in dramatic Bollywood fashion, to stop the wedding! Finally, the priest excused himself from the conversation, put the phone down and went back to the worried couple. He threw the ring into the bucket again and this time Roshan allowed Lakshmi to find and pull it out. You could see that this made her happy.

The priest kept them walking around and finally they were married. Man and wife. Bride and groom. I couldn't help but think of this cheesy episode of *Full House* I saw as a kid where everybody goes to a Greek wedding involving John Stamos' character. They walk around in a circle too to get married but for some reason end up nullifying the wedding by walking backwards around the circle. If only I could nullify the events of the past few months by walking backwards, I would. By slipping off this cast and picking myself off the bottom of Emily's fire escape and flying upwards across her ledge, my arms pinwheeling for balance. Helping my father up from the ice where he slipped and fell, taking him to the hospital. After the initial shock of my return home from hospital, he had not said two words to me, spooked. I thought of that time on the beach, my earliest memory. The white sands and the sparkling water. The rustle of wax paper, inexpertly tied, against my leg. My father had not even touched me this time, refused to sign my cast. I caught his eye and he quickly looked away; involuntarily, the urge swelled up in me to have him kiss my foot, to suck all the bad blood of the past few months away from it. He might never touch me again and I felt the loss, as if we had momentarily switched places; I was the parent and he was the son; I had lost him forever. He depended on me to introduce him, to inculcate him, to the new country. I had failed. But how would I know how to do my duty? Who was there to teach *me*? I should have been there, for him, when he slipped and fell. If I had to choose now between only having my leg broken again and going through what I went through with Emily, I would choose to have my leg broken.

As if she could sense my melancholy thoughts, my mother descended upon me. "What's the matter, Thambi?" she asked, pressing my shoulders and smiling. She was genuinely smiling and I could see the tears, threatening to roll any minute, streak her phantom face. "One day this will all be for you," she said. "Don't despair. You will meet your match. Someone will help you bring the best out of yourself. So what if you saw that white girl? It's over and done with. We all make our mistakes. If it was a year ago, I would have been furious and bewildered at you too. But since your father feels that way, what's the point in my echoing him? I never did really understand that man; I'll have to work on him. He needs a lot of help and patience. As for you...you're my baby son."

With this, she began to cry freely and hugged me as best as she could while standing above me. I cried too, not for what I'd done, but because I'd been changed by it. It scared me, the lack of control I held, that anyone held, over our own lives. Looking around the hall, I saw the single girls in their saris, seated with their families, for the first time. I wondered whether any of them would marry me; whether any of them could take a wretch like me?

I saw my mother as the hard lined woman cracking the telephone receiver down upon its base for one last time, and then the image evaporated. In time, the bitterness and regret vanished, and I felt a weakened love and wonder for everyone in my life. Roshan was going to vanish from me, from all of us, very soon. I thought about our estranged relationship as two women from Lakshmi's side held a vessel and flame in front of the couple and moved it in a clockwise manner, blessing them.

He was always the older one, and as a kid, I had looked up to him for guidance and example. I had admired him only by virtue of the fact that he was older. As I grew, I quickly picked up that he wasn't smarter or wiser; he simply did what was expected of him and never talked back or thought for himself. My mother, though she was content with this, did not respect him. She liked me, and he had always resented me for this; no matter what he did, it was never quite good enough. In my heart of hearts, I had derided him and gone my own way, and this is where things had come to now. What incentive could Roshan possibly have to stay devoted to us? He had traded one stern taskmaster, my mother, for another. I was going to get stuck with her and my father by myself. Perhaps this would bring us closer but I doubted it.

"Come," said my mother, "let's go up on the stage." She drew me up by my shoulders and I, uncomfortably, struggled with my crutches to get up. I limped with her, arm in arm, towards the dais. As if she was my date, it felt like the most natural thing in the world. Our slow process to the institutionalized ceremony designed to encircle desire that was coming to a conclusion upon its stage.

"Ladies and gentlemen," said the cellphone wielding priest, talking into a microphone, "Mr. and Mrs. Navaratnam! God bless your families and children. Long life, good health, and happiness to you. May you receive everything you desire from the Gods. They will give you everything. Congratulations!"

The DJ pumped in the electronic pipes and cymbals and the celebratory music got underway. I could smell the curries from the hot plates that were being served outside the hall. A dosai maker had set up a grill to spread the mix and fry up dosais for those who wanted them. Roshan and Lakshmi genuflected in turn to both our parents and hers and they were now married. I joined the others in lining up to give them my good wishes and congratulate them. My mother stooped and picked up some flowers so that I could throw them and join in with everybody else. There were still many hours to go, but

Roshan and Lakshmi looked relieved, radiant, and sated as they sat there in their wooden thrones like royalty who have achieved something.

That was a few weeks ago and Roshan and Lakshmi, who have now returned from their honeymoon, are settling into their new home, close to her parents. Despite my father's objections, Lakshmi's parents helped them out generously and continue to help them out. He was full of bluster and vehemence and righteous indignation but none of these things could compete with the steady dissenters he met with whenever he raised his objections. He was outnumbered. Roshan had moved out just after our father had arrived and will never have to deal with him in the quantities that my mother will. They seem to have struck up a rocky balance. We are in the long process of waiting to see what will come of his refugee claim. Right now, he is looking for odd jobs where he can get paid under the table. He wants to move us out of the apartment, into a house, but you need money for that.

The leg? It's coming along nicely, thanks. My mother offers to wash me but I don't need that kind of attention at this point in my life, do I? I've figured out a way I can allow myself to lower my body into the bathtub and leave my right leg with the cast hanging out. Then I slowly wash myself. What I wouldn't give to be able to take a shower! Maybe there's some way I can waterproof and seal my cast in a plastic bag or something and take a shower; I'll have to work on that. I've gotten really good at moving with the crutches now. Three appendages provide stability, and as long as I'm careful where I place the crutches, I can move pretty fast on them with a rolling gait. The last set of x-rays from the hospital show that the bones are healing well and I definitely won't need surgery as long as everything continues to heal nicely. There's some pain and stiffness but the doctor says that there will always be pain and stiffness. If only they could make x-rays that would peer inside men's souls; if they could peer into my fraudulent heart and tell me what I should do to flush it out! I walk about with this stiffness that extends from my leg to my heart. People always make way for me on the streetcar or at the supermarket. I've even begun to send out resumés and look for a new job.

I couldn't go back to my old job, of course. I try not to think of Emily. She didn't have a permanent desk there and was going to leave anyway, but there were just too many memories. Even if we had previously avoided each other, the certainty that I would go over to her place and make love to her pale body hovered around and settled like a fine cloud, like late afternoon sunshine bathing me in light. It gave a rise to my day. I don't know how to get hold of her now. The only contact information I had was her Toronto number which is no longer in service. I have the Nipple of course that she gave me, that useless hunk of plastic like a sex toy in the shape of a white stylized breast. Perhaps I should give it to the priest who's always on his cellphone? I curse myself now for not having set it up on the Nipplework when she gave it to me so that I could have seen what music and other things she'd put on it for me. With time, whenever my thoughts float upon that ugly piece of plastic, I come to think of it like her. Aesthetic, cool to the touch, unblemished on the outside. Impenetrable, like an informational black hole; I'm not really sure what's on the inside. I wish I could take an x-ray machine to the Nipple and see what's contained inside it. I feel that if I could penetrate that mysterious white box, I would see inside Emily Vale and ultimately, what she was to me. Perhaps nothing. Perhaps a phantom of myself. Perhaps everything.

My parents never talk of her. But they do bring up marriage, as does every guest and relative who comes by for a visit. My parents pull the wedding (or 'weeding') album out. I have a hard time looking at those photos, and my parents and everybody else's questions about marriage form a steady insistence, like heavy rain or the water treatment method of torture. *Drip Drip Drip. Marriage Marriage Marriage.*

We come back to the question of why I launched myself from Emily's fire escape. Was I escaping a fire or jumping back into one? Was I jumping away from my old life or falling back to it? My suspicion, my dreaded thought which I have not shared with anyone, save you, is that I was jumping onto the panic button as hard as I could. Without even realizing it, without even thinking through what it meant, I started the process of blaring the siren; not simply welding my palm to the console but launching my whole body upon it. I will be thirty this year. I don't have much money and I don't know what I'm doing with my life. I don't trust myself not to give in, over time, to arranged marriage, the panic button of Hindu romance. In my worst hours, I imagine that it is the real reason why I broke my leg: to test possible marriage candidates and applicants; only someone truly caring enough to replace my mother would replace my mother!

In the middle of the night, my leg hurts. I can't scratch it, and I get up in terror and find for myself the container of painkillers. Sometimes I take a painkiller even when it isn't strictly necessary, to take care of another kind of pain if you know what I mean. The opiates numb my senses. Gone is the freewheeling confidence at the beginning of the last night that I saw Emily. Back comes the freefalling sense of abandon as I launch through the air. Will I ever meet someone like her again, unencumbered by tradition, cleanly inserting herself between pleasure and whatever the past held? Will I meet anyone again? I still look forward to breaking off this cast in a month and getting back on my own two feet. Will I become a new person or is Roshan the only butterfly to fly this deadly cocoon? I don't know. Should I hold out or bring my palm down on the panic button, plain and clear for all to see?

You're a doctor, the profession that my culture holds in highest regard and esteem. Maybe you could tell me what I should do.

What do you think I should do?

Thanks to Ed Yanofsky, Pete Cram, Rob Shoub, and especially Luciano Iacobelli.

Other Quattro Novellas